Proof of Existence

Aubrey

Antonio C. Mendez

To choke work through the madness

For Mom,
My provenance of valor

Prologue

"BEING a teacher suits you," someone from the group said. "Maybe after saving the world, we can be substitutes for real." The four of them were standing inside a windowed hallway watching outside. The youngest, a small girl, had her hands raised against the glass with her eyes shut so tight her head ached.

"I can't stand the way they stare at me," the tallest of the group responded. "Like, what? I have all the answers. Most of what I said was gibberish. What do I know about anything?" She did little to hide her annoyance. "I do like the clothes, though."

"That's what I meant," the one who spoke first responded. He was a wide man with a smile to match. A young man stepped up from the middle of the group.

"Guys," he commanded. "Focus. We've been preparing for this moment these last few days. We can't mess this up." The boy took his attention to the girl and put his hand on her shoulder. "Can you do this?" he asked.

"This will be the biggest I've ever made," she responded, straining through her concentration. She took a step back and regained her composure. "Let me try again."

"We can find another way," the boy said. "Don't hurt yourself." There was real concern in his voice. The girl felt it, and this made her more determined to get it right. Again, she lifted her hands to the glass and concentrated.

They waited a few moments. The group watched as a wall of concrete formed just outside the windows. It spread like fire until it blocked the view. It took almost a minute to cover the entire building. Although the display was amazing, the young man looked down at his watch. He had a schedule to keep.

"Great work," he said with sincerity. "You two go lock all the doors and don't forget the rubber strips on the cracks. We've only got a few minutes before we get started." Without hesitation, the two eldest of the group rushed out of the hallway. They disappeared behind loud metal doors.

"That should be it," the girl said. Her voice shook from the strain. Truthfully, he felt bad for her. This wasn't where she should be. None of them should be here.

"Hey," he said with a soft voice. "I know that was hard. I owe you. You are incredible, truly. Remember, none of this would be possible without you. I will need you later, but for now, go to one of the buildings in the back and get some rest. You've earned it."

In response, the girl managed a nod. She exited through the door that led outside and disappeared beneath the rubble she created. Each step she took looked as if her legs could not bear it.

"I'll take it from here," he said to her.

Protectors

AUBREY
October 15, 1999
[6: 40 A.M.]

JUDGMENT IS COMING, ARE YOU READY?

These were the words Aubrey kept seeing on the white walls of her new school. The posters were unsettling, but she liked the message. It was Friday morning, and she was taking her frustration out on her jammed locker.

Earlier, she and her mom got into an argument. With a new school comes new experiences and new lives, but that wasn't what Aubrey wanted. Her mom, on the other hand, thought it would be good for her. At least that's what she kept saying. She just wanted to justify her selfish decisions. As soon as she finished formulating the thought, she regretted it. She understood her mother and father were going through a divorce. They just seemed to forget they had a daughter.

This was Aubrey's first day. The hall was lit with fluorescent lights, revealing a long stretch of a high school hallway. The lockers were all a rusty brown color and the floor was a dull white, just like every other school she'd been to. Sure, she liked the forest setting more than the swamp they used to live in, but she liked her friends from her old school. She was not looking forward to meeting new people; she was bad at it and knew she was. The locker still wasn't budging. She leaned her head against her locker. It was going to be a long day.

"Do you need some help?" a voice asked. Startled, she quickly looked over at the person. It was a boy about her age. He was tall and thin. He was wearing a tight leather jacket and blue jeans with blue chucks. His face was gorgeous and his smile, seductive. It was his eyes that she liked the most though, they looked silver.

"No," she said shyly. She looked back down at the combination dial and started putting in the numbers again.

"Let me help." The boy seemed to glide in front of her. His shoulder brushed her cheek. The feeling of him being so close, close enough that they were practically hugging, made her stomach flutter. She stumbled off behind him a bit and watched him open the locker.

"Are you new here?" he asked. He must have noticed that it was empty, she thought.

"Yeah, we just got settled in last night." She kept her sentences short, trying not to let her voice shake. Over her shoulder was her messenger bag. She reached inside it and put a few folders and notebooks inside the locker.

"Well," he said, taking a step back. "That is interesting." The way he talked was as if he wasn't responding to what she just said, but rather his mind was somewhere else.

"What's your name?" he asked.

"Aubrey Hammond, what's yours?"

"Stephen." She noticed he didn't add his last name.

"It's nice to meet you." She extended her arm out for a handshake as she said the words.

Taking her hand, he said, "Agreed." They locked eyes during the exchange, but it was like he couldn't see her. It was like his mind was formulating a plan, or searching for an answer to a question that was never asked.

"I need to go do something before school starts," he said, releasing his firm but considerate grip. "It really was nice meeting you." He turned away and walked down the hall, around the corner, and out of sight. This person himself, Stephen, might be the sole reason she liked her new school. With her messenger bag around her shoulder, containing a notebook and pens, and her schedule in hand, she walked in the opposite direction.

She walked to the back of the school with intention to go to her homeroom, so she could sit and wait for the rest of the school to come alive. She was walking through the long windowed hallway when she heard a kind of swooshing sound coming from outside. Glancing out of the window, she could see the outlines of trees, the forest she admired.

Suddenly, a bright light consumed the windows. It seemed to hit her with a small bit of force, knocking her off balance. It looked to her like the sun crashed into the earth, but much smaller. Her eyes shut in reaction, and when she opened them it was gone.

Aubrey looked out at the world, confused. As her eyes adjusted to the darkness, she noticed there was now a mound of dirt where she thought she saw the orb of light. Did something really crash into the ground? At the end of the hall, there was a door that went outside in the direction the light seemed to come from. She ran to it and exited the building.

The cold air hit her shoulders first, then her face. Her jacket was in her locker. A long sleeve and baggy jeans didn't do much to block the cold. As she approached the mound of dirt, the air grew warmer. She felt a tingling at the tip of her fingers, like the moment before a doorknob shocks you from static. She took a step onto the dirt and peered down. Dust floated out into the cold air but before her was a hole, about the size of a backyard swimming pool. Faintly, the outline of a man started to form.

"Is someone down there?" she called out. For a moment there was silence. Then she heard a cough.

"Hello?" she shouted down. The dust cleared, revealing two people. A young man and woman. The boy was kneeling next to the girl. The condition of the girl was bad. Her chest looked as if someone had taken a blade and hacked away at her as if someone had been desperately trying to reach her heart. She was covered in blood, lots of blood. The boy didn't look hurt, only out of breath, gasping for air.

"Help…" the boy tried to get out through his deep breathing. Aubrey understood and jumped into the ditch. She reached the two, getting a better look at the boy. He had brown skin, black hair, and was just a little taller than her. Aubrey looked at his hands. No blood. Then to his shirt. No blood there either.

"What happened?" Aubrey asked as she put her arms around the woman's legs. They both seemed to know what to do without talking. The boy stumbled around to her head and lifted the rest of her.

"I don't know, I found her like this," the boy said. They began working on getting her out of the ditch. It was a struggle as the boy went over the dirt mounds. Aubrey wasn't sure if the girl was even alive. She was limp, but warm to the touch.

"Do you know who she is?" Aubrey asked as they were crossing through the yard.

"She looks like Holly," the boy said, out of breath. "But with all this blood on her, it's hard to tell." They entered the hallway and stopped for a moment. It occurred to Aubrey that she didn't know where the nurse's office was, but she assumed that it was near the front of the school. The boy was looking at her, waiting for directions. She motioned down the hall.

They entered the hall where her locker was and rushed past a blur of brown doors. They took a left and Aubrey could see the office doors on the right. Entering the room, they found it empty. There was a sign on the wall that pointed toward the nurse. Together they carried her down a small hallway and found the door that led to the nurse's office. Aubrey hit the door handle and the door flew open. There was no nurse.

"What do we do now?" the boy asked. Aubrey motioned for them to set the girl down on one of the beds. The moment the girl's body hit the bed the boy stumbled back and fell to the floor. Aubrey leaned against the wall.

"So, who are you?" the man asked her, finally able to breathe.

"I'm Aubrey Hammond. Who are you?"

"I'm Manny Navarro." They rested in a moment of silence. "Where am I?" he asked. She thought it was a weird question.

"Do you mean the name of the school? It's Aspen Grove High School." She could tell that she was revealing her confusion to him.

"I ask because I can't remember anything except for my name." She could see in his eyes that he was trying hard to remember. It was the way he was staring over at the girl like he really didn't know who she was but wanted to.

"Do you know her?" she asked. "You said earlier, she looks like Holly. Is that her name?"

"No," he responded confidently. "That's not Holly. I don't know who she is." The way he was looking at her made Aubrey feel uncomfortable. It was like he was hiding something he was feeling. He clenched his jaw from the frustration. Aubrey didn't know what to say to him. She was certain that the woman that was lying on the bed was alive which, to her, was a very good thing. She watched her chest rise and fall and could hear the hoarse rumble of breathing.

Manny closed his eyes and let his head fall back. He was looking straight up at the ceiling when he started talking, "You know how people pray that one day we'll wake up and that this will all just be a dream?" He paused as he cleared his throat. "Well, what if this is a dream and, like in a real dream, we wake up right before the best part?"

The question seemed random. "I'm not sure how to answer... but look, she really needs help. I'm going to do what I can. See if you can find a phone or someone to help us." Manny nodded and stood to leave. Aubrey watched him. He was tall and built like a soldier, and he walked with purpose. *Could she trust him?*

Although he was the only one around when Aubrey found them, he had no blood on him. With how much blood was on the girl, her attacker was sure to be just as covered. It couldn't be Manny, but she didn't know him.

The girl on the bed moved onto her side, whimpering in pain. She had to still be unconscious. If she was awake, she would surely be screaming. Aubrey walked over to a cabinet that had the words FIRST AID. She was looking for peroxide, gauze, and bandages to cover the wound. Inside there was an array of different supplies. She grabbed what she needed along with a towel and turned toward the girl.

The blood that painted the girl looked fresh but was beginning to harden. It was in her hair and down her body to her ankles. She was only wearing tattered and charred underwear, nothing else. How this girl wasn't dead escaped Aubrey. With the items in her hands, she made her way back to her side.

The scene was hard for her to look at. There was a gaping wound across her chest. The exposed muscle and tissue pulsed. She thought the girl looked malnourished and very pale. *Where had she come from, and why was she so brutally harmed?* Aubrey just wanted to know the story. There had to be a reason.

Aubrey stripped off the little clothing the girl had on. It smelled of ashes and fire. She had a clear view of the wound. It looked like someone took a chainsaw to get to her heart, but something about that assumption seemed wrong. A chainsaw would cause tearing of the entire area, but it looked like her chest had been ripped off rather than hacked away at. Aubrey soaked the towel with peroxide and wiped it at the drying blood. The sudden cold must've woken the girl up because she opened her eyes and looked directly into Aubrey's.

Staring up at her were red-orange eyes like the color of autumn leaves, soft, amber, and broken. There was a fear in her eyes that made Aubrey recoil. She could tell, unlike Manny, whether he was telling the truth, this girl remembered everything. It was written all over her face. The girl grabbed her wrist and pulled. She was attempting to sit up.

"What are you doing?" Aubrey yelled, holding her down. She watched as the girl moved her mouth as if to talk, but no sound came out. Realizing she couldn't speak, the girl motioned toward the door.

"Why are you trying to leave?" Aubrey asked, getting frustrated. The girl tried to talk again. This time, managing only moans and coughs. The girl must've become frustrated as well, as she started hitting her forearm. The cries soon turned into weeping as the girl turned her head away and retracted her arms to her side. It was like she was unaware of the pain as she closed her eyes to suffer alone. Aubrey was standing beside her now, unsure of what to do.

"I know that you're hurt," Aubrey said. "And I know that I don't know you, but I want you to know that I will take care of you. All I want to do is clean you up. Manny went to get help. He'll be back soon." *She hoped.*

The girl nodded between wiping her eyes. Aubrey began cleaning the areas with clumps of dirt still embedded into her skin. From the carnage, Aubrey assumed there would be bruises or cuts but the only injury seemed to be her chest. "What happened to you?" The question came out of her mouth without thinking.

The girl's eyes flared as if her soul ignited. It was pain. It was anger. The story was there within her eyes but not her voice. Her mouth opened to talk, to scream, to cry, but again nothing. It occurred to Aubrey that maybe the cause of the wound could have been so traumatic that it took her voice. "Can you talk?" Aubrey asked. The girl shook her head.

"Can you write?" The girl shook her head again. "Why not?" With that question, the girl slammed her fists into the bed as she shook her head. The girl looked like she could be the same age as her, maybe a little older. *Who was this girl?*

After cleaning what she could see, Aubrey began to dress the wound. First, she placed strips of gauze over the exposed area. It turned red as it soaked into her. With another layer, it slowed down. Then she motioned for the girl to lift herself. She sat up and Aubrey wrapped the bandage across her chest and shoulders. She forgot the tape, she realized. The sound of her heart beating pulsated in her ears when she went back to the medicine cabinet. The tape was on the bottom shelf. She turned back to the girl.

The injured girl was standing in front of the sink staring into the mirror. Aubrey stopped and watched as the girl moved her hand to her chest. This must have been the first time she noticed. The girl flinched when she touched the bandages. Aubrey's mind went to her own feelings. What would she be thinking if she discovered someone or something had ripped away her chest?

"Do you remember what happened?" Aubrey asked. The girl didn't look over or show any indication of hearing her. That was fine. As curious as she was, this wasn't about Aubrey.

"I just need to tape the ends down so your wound doesn't get infected." Again the girl showed no sign that she heard her. She just stared into the mirror.

Aubrey grabbed the end that hung from her back and pulled it tight. She tore a few pieces of tape off the roll and applied them. The girl stood there unmoving. It was like her soul was dead but her body didn't know it yet. When she was done she stood back unsure of what to do next. The girl was still standing in front of the mirror with her eyes only partly open. Her amber eyes were distant, dead.

Slowly, as though her body was broken, the girl turned to face her. Maybe it was the emptiness that made them impressionable, but regardless of the reason, they moved something within Aubrey. Pure emotion moved through her body causing her to tear up. She felt sorry for her. If it were Aubrey in her place she would have curled up and accepted death. There was something about this girl that screamed freedom and life, but the way she looked told a different story. A beautiful contradiction stood in front of her. The girl snapped out of the trance and looked at Aubrey with eyes filled with concern. She could tell that the girl wanted to say something, anything, but she was unable to.

"You don't have to talk," Aubrey said. "I will help you. You may not be able to tell me what happened but that doesn't matter. Once the teachers and staff show up we'll get you some real help." The girl's eyes lit up with words but none slipped through her lips. "Manny, the guy who found you, he said your name might be Holly. Is that your name?"

The time that passed for the girl to respond seemed unusually long, but a few moments later she shook her head.

"We'll figure that out later," Aubrey said. "I've done all I can do right now." Her voice echoed off of the room's tiles. The words seemed to linger in the air while she waited for some type of response from the girl. When Aubrey turned to exit the room the girl grabbed her wrist.

The grip was tight and reassuring. This told Aubrey that she appreciated the kindness and generosity that she was showing her, but for an unknown reason, Aubrey was unable to understand the feelings. She couldn't put a label to the emotions that were flowing into her chest, the emotions that were making her feel warm and relaxed. Little did she know, this moment, this comforting, homely moment, would be the last she ever had.

From a speaker above the two girls heard a loud bell that signified the beginning of the school day and soon after a man took to a microphone to talk to the entire student body.

[7: 45 A.M.]

Adjudication of Now

MANNY
October 15, 1999
[7: 30 A.M.]

Manny stumbled through shoulders and book bags trying to follow the kid he just met. Students seemed to pour into the school through the very cracks that held it together. Manny could hear their conversations. They talked of class and of their peers. Both subjects were being spoken of negatively. In the halls, Manny could feel the negativity, he could almost see it. The only sense of positive emotions was coming from his guide. He was taking strides like he owned the school and the students attending. They all acknowledged his existence by waving or smiling in his direction. Manny wondered if he might be popular.

"The office is just up here," the guide said back to Manny. They rounded a corner that took them to the main office again. Anxiety swept over Manny as he saw the sign with the word NURSE on it. He didn't want to see Aubrey or the other girl again. Drake stepped into the office alone, while Manny hesitated.

"Hey," the boy said back to him. "I get it, man. On my first day, I wanted to just leave too. The people here can be a little overwhelming sometimes. Especially if it's your first day. Where would you have gone if I hadn't stopped you?" Without giving Manny a chance to answer, the boy said, "That's weird."

"What's weird?" Manny asked, getting the sudden urge to run.

"There aren't any administrators. Usually, they're all over the place, but no one's here at the front desk, and the offices in the back look empty." The young man stood at the secretary's desk and thought for a moment. Then he looked down and grabbed two papers.

"What's your last name, Manny," the boy asked.

"Navarro," he replied. "I don't mean to be rude, but what is your name?"

"Oh gosh, I'm the rude one!" He extended his hand. "I'm Drake. It looks like there's a schedule for you and another student named Michelle. Here." Manny stepped into the office and grabbed the card out of his hand. He looked it over, hoping to maybe see an address or some other form of identification, but there was nothing.

"It looks like we have a pretty similar schedule," the kid said to Manny. "I can take you to your first class. We've got that together."

"You know a lot about the school?" Manny asked. Something didn't feel right to him. Not just him not remembering anything, but about the boy, and this place.

"What kind of question is that?" Drake laughed. "It's just dumb high school. We've got everything you'd expect. Bad food. Bad people. Boring classes. Overbearing teachers that take their classes too seriously. It's all honestly, very boring. Is something wrong?"

"I just feel like something's wrong," Manny said, wishing that he hadn't. A part of him felt he should keep to himself. Drake was giving him a funny look.

"Well," Drake said, moving toward the door. "You can stay here if you want. Maybe someone will show up soon, or you can come with me to your first class. Look, you've got a schedule, don't you? You're obviously supposed to be here."

"Yeah," Manny said. "I'll go with you."

The two of them walked out into the hall, which was now empty. All the chaos seemed to just vanish. The students must have all been in class.

The off-white walls did well to make a person feel like they were in an asylum, especially with the fluorescent lights. With empty halls, it looked like the school had once been used for a prison or concentration camp. There were posters down and up the halls with the statement JUDGMENT IS COMING, ARE YOU READY? He thought it was odd, but that was the only thought he had about it. The paint, Manny assumed, was used to try and cover up the building's past. With a past comes scars that are everlasting and feelings like energy, the type of energy that could never be harnessed or transformed.

Something about the hall made him think that he had maybe once been to a school and was a student. He must've been a teenager, or at least looked like one with the way Drake was treating him. It was comforting to know that there were people that would take care of him the way that Drake was.

From overhead, the announcement speakers kicked on with a loud beep. Manny stopped walking behind Drake as the voice began talking. The halls suddenly felt fortified and small. The lights seemed to dim with every word, with every syllable spoken Manny's very soul seemed to crumble. It was like breaking down the very cells of his mind and reconstructing them with the words, with the voice. Drake had stopped walking and was staring up at one of the speakers. Time seemed to freeze, leaving Manny with a sense of dread. The words were cold and precise like the person speaking had thought of these words their entire life, and only right then could they formulate what needed to be said.

The voice said, "The pillars of society reside in your hands. They are the very bones that form the structure of your skeleton. There is a fire charring your flesh, this is your soul, and from ashes to dust and birth to death, when the light fades it will turn black. You were resting, waiting, planning, but now your curse will set you free. Pandora had hers, and now I have mine."

A second beep sounded, and the voice was gone leaving Manny and Drake in the hall with a feeling of isolation. Both of the two boys felt it, but neither one moved or said a word. Their eyes were still fixed on the speaker that was right above their heads. It stared back at them like a single eye in the sky, far away, silently judging.

"I feel it too," Drake said, his voice shaking. It was like he was scared to admit what he was feeling. Manny wondered if Drake could possibly be feeling exactly what he was feeling. It was too unique, divine almost. "I don't recognize the voice. I wonder if a new student did the announcements or if they hired a new faculty member. Either way, that was definitely creepy, to say the least."

Drake started walking again. Hesitantly, Manny followed. The experience made him uneasy. The words seemed to mean a lot more to him than they did to Drake unless he was just not revealing his actual feelings. Manny could feel the words burn his skull, not just burn, but sear. He felt like the man had spoken directly to him.

It would be easier, for now, to go along with Drake. If Manny were to resist following this schedule, he feared he would appear suspicious. He would bide his time and wait for his memories to come back.

"You ready for class?"

[7: 58 A.M.]

Students

AUBREY
October 15, 1999
[7: 47 A.M.]

Aubrey exited the nurse's office looking for a lost and found bin. The announcement that just played made her feel uneasy. *Why would someone say those things?* To her, it was a threat, a warning, or maybe a promise. She walked down to the front of the office, looking under desks and inside closets. Laying on one of the desks, she found a schedule like hers. This was where she had gotten hers earlier, but it was alone. Someone had to have put this here afterward. It had the name Michelle in the top margins. She grabbed it.

Turning around, she saw a box full of jackets with the letters L and F painted lazily on the front. Rummaging through, she managed to find a shirt and a pair of jeans. It would have to do. She ran back with the clothes in hand and entered the nurse's office again. The smell of blood and dirt washed over her.

The girl was cleaning the cot she had been lying on with a wet rag. She even made a pile of trash from the wrappers the medical supplies had come in. She was cleaning her mess. It seemed odd to be concerned with.

"I brought you some clothes," Aubrey said, walking to her. "You don't have to clean that. I can take care of it." The girl ignored her, finishing the job. She stood in front of Aubrey. There was a different look on her face. A determined one. *What changed?* The girl took the clothes and pulled them over her body. The clothes were a little big, but she didn't seem to mind.

"I found this too." Aubrey took the schedule from her pocket and handed it over. The girl read it over. "Were you supposed to start school today?" Aubrey asked. The girl shook her head at first, but as if she changed her mind, nodded.

"So, you're Michelle?" Aubrey asked. The girl nodded. "I feel like we should try to find you an adult. That Manny guy never came back, and I don't really trust him anyways." Michelle grabbed Aubrey by the shoulders and shook her. She shook her head again.

"You don't want me to get you help?" Aubrey asked, confused. Michelle shook her head. There was a sense of urgency in her eyes. "Fine. I won't. What are you going to do then? I feel like maybe you should go home at least. We can call your parents from the office."

Michelle, still holding onto Aubrey's shoulders, pushed her away out of frustration. The girl seemed to try to scream as a muffled sound passed through her throat. She pulled the schedule up and pointed to it. Aubrey herself began to get frustrated.

"I'm just trying to help you," she said with too much anger. "What do you want to do? Go to class? You need medical attention. You could get an infection and you've lost a lot of blood. I'm surprised you're even alive if I'm being honest. Those bandages won't last long." Aubrey's voice came to a sudden rest but the harsh tone echoed off the wet tiles.

Composed, Michelle pushed the schedule closer to Aubrey's face and pointed at it again. There was no reasoning with someone who couldn't talk.

"Fine. We can go to class because everything is just dandy." Aubrey didn't try to hide the sarcasm. "We have the same schedule anyways. I'll be able to keep an eye on you."

Satisfied, Michelle took her hand out of Aubrey's face. This girl made no sense to Aubrey. She wished she could know what she was thinking.

"We should get going then," Aubrey said. "I think class started already."

The two girls left the nurse's office and headed to the front of the office. It occurred to Aubrey that she didn't grab the girl any shoes. They stopped for a moment at the lost and found bin and scavenged some old boots that seemed to fit. It was notably quiet in the office. Aubrey looked around for any signs of life. It was empty. Aubrey took her own schedule from her pocket and read the room number.

"Follow me," she said to her new friend. They walked down empty halls until they reached their classroom. Standing outside the door, they could hear the murmur of a teacher lazily lecturing. Aubrey opened the door.

"Sorry," she said shyly. The teacher paused making eye contact with a glare. Aubrey looked back at Michelle as if to say, here's our chance to get some help. Michelle turned down the offer by shaking her head. The two girls walked into the room and found seats near the front still empty.

The teacher resumed the lecture, explaining the concept of utilitarianism. The whole while, Aubrey's mind was on Michelle. Who was this girl and why was she with Manny? Where did she come from?

An hour or so passed and they found themselves back out in the hall surrounded by a crowd of teenagers.

"Our next class is just down the hall," Aubrey directed. As they began to walk, Manny rounded the corner accompanied by another student. As their eyes locked, Manny stopped walking. It was his guilt, Aubrey thought. She ran up to him, pushing through book bags and shoulders.

"Where did you go?" she yelled at him. She didn't wait for him to respond. "Michelle was waiting for help. I had to take care of her, alone." The other student with Manny spoke first.

"Who are you?" he said. Aubrey ignored him.

"Are you gonna say anything?" she said, shoving Manny's shoulder.

"I went to look for help," he responded, annoyed. "I couldn't find any adults and when I went

back to find you two, you guys were gone."

"Liar," Aubrey shouted. "We were in that nurse's office for a while. You never came back. Who even are you? Why did I find you with Michelle?" Manny pulled his own schedule from his pocket.

"I'm a student here," he said, shoving it in her face. "As I said before, I don't remember anything. Did she say anything? Does she know why I was with her?" He asked Aubrey, but he looked over at Michelle who was walking up behind Aubrey, for protection.

"She can't talk," she responded, calming her voice. "But you remember everything right?" Michelle nodded.

"Did he hurt you?" Aubrey asked, feeling relieved that the questions she wanted to know the answer to were finally being asked. To her surprise, Michelle shook her head. Now all three teenagers were looking at Michelle.

"Do you know who hurt you?" Manny asked this time. Michelle watched as the man's eyes lit up with the question. She hesitated to answer but eventually nodded her head.

"Is he out in the woods or somewhere around here still?" Aubrey asked. The thought scared her. Someone that brutally cruel could be lurking around. Michelle shook her head. Aubrey asked if she was sure, and she shook her head harder.

"Just talk!" Manny shouted. It was sudden. Other students looked over to see what was happening. Michelle grabbed onto Aubrey.

"You don't talk to her like that." Aubrey's words were stern. "This is done. She's been through a lot. She doesn't have to do anything." Aubrey walked through the two teenagers while Michelle followed. They walked to their next class in silence. They found a couple of seats in the back.

As other students walked in, they would spot the couple and begin to whisper. Aubrey noticed but didn't care. She kept thinking about Manny. It was odd that he didn't seem at all concerned about Michelle's injuries. Between the girl's concern about attending class and Manny's ignorance of the whole situation, she felt she was the only sane person in the whole building. These weren't normal high school problems, she thought to herself.

Soon the teacher walked into the room and started talking about the day's lesson. Aubrey tried to pay attention but got as far as learning that light is made of small particles called photons. All that had happened to her today was swirling through her mind. All at once, the lecture began and ended with another hour passing by. The bell rang and the sound of twenty students opening their book bags filled the room. At the same time, a voice cut through the noise.

"Why are you acting like that?" Aubrey had been lost in thought but the question brought her back to the classroom. Before her stood a girl gripping a book so tight her knuckles had turned white. She was looking down at Aubrey with fierce eyes, her black hair blocking a flickering light casting a shadow over her angry face.

"What?" Aubrey responded, not able to find words. This seemed to anger the girl.

"I watched you in the hall," the girl said, throwing her hand in Michelle's direction. "You aren't better than her. What do you want? Is someone supposed to praise you for protecting her? You made a scene for attention. I see you. I know what you are."

Aubrey watched the girl turn her back and leave the room. The girl didn't give her a chance to respond. Nothing here made sense to her. She glanced over to Michelle who was looking back at her. She was laughing.

[9: 45 AM]

Destiny's Collapse

ASTERIA
October 15, 1999
[3: 29 P.M.]

"This doesn't make any sense," Asteria Griffin muttered to herself as she walked around to the other side of the massive cement structure. She pulled the directions she had written down from her overcoat. This is where the school should be but it looks like the dumpsite for old concrete.

When she woke up in her car a few hours ago she thought this place would help her understand. This was another dead end and not his old high school. She noticed that the cement pile went on for a while and also that there was no hint of there being a school on any side. Nothing about this made sense to her, not the giant crater behind the cement pile, nor the parking lot full of cars.

She put the directions back in her pocket and walked back to her car. She left it running with the door open. Slipping inside, her hand found the knob that controlled the heat and she cranked it. The tips of her finger stung as she raised them to the warm air. It made her remember the last time she saw him. It was cold then too.

That was only five days ago, she thought. Two years changed him, two years of constant torture. Not intentional torture, she tried to justify herself, it was necessary torture. It needed to be done in order to save him from everyone. Or was it to save everyone from him?

She'd spent seven months with him and she knew she wasn't the same person as before. She couldn't even remember. She didn't want to. Instead, she was in her car staring at a pile of rocks.

This didn't make any sense.

This location was verified twice by her sources. A school should be here. She left her car with it still running. This time she was intent on uncovering the truth. Something in her gut told her the whole situation was wrong. She stood staring at the cement. It was gray, just as it should be, but it was an unusually large pile of cement. Her phone vibrated in her pocket.

"Hello?" she answered the call, still staring at the cement. "No, I haven't gotten any leads... I know... The one lead I did get seems to be a dead end but I have a feeling... It's just a feeling... I know I shouldn't leave this up to my feelings... Yes... Who knows him better than me? I was his therapist. I was his handler... Kip, just calm down. I know what's at stake... Stop... Listen to me, I will figure this out... Okay, I'll call you when I get any more information... I know, I know... Bye."

This was the fifth time he's called today. She didn't like it when Castle checked in on her. Sometimes she felt like they treated her like a child. Kip wasn't so bad, it was Ronald that made her feel nervous. It was the way he talked... She took her mind off of it. She didn't want to think about it. She walked around to the back of the structure to look again at the crater.

There weren't signs of explosives being set off or an excavation being performed so she concluded something must have fallen or someone dug this. She looked to the sky, what could have fallen? She looked back to the crater and noticed a reddish tint in parts of the dirt. Taking a closer look she realized it was blood.

From her coat pocket, she took out a bag and knelt down. She scooped some of the dirt into the container, sealed it, and then put it back in her coat pocket. It was curious to her that in her search for the boy, she would find a trail of blood. Her thoughts were interrupted by a muffled bang that came from behind her.

Asteria looked back at the cement. Parts of it shimmered in the light as if someone mixed in crystals or glass. *Was that a gunshot?* In the cold, in the silence, she wondered if she imagined the sound. She walked up to the smoothest section and rubbed her hand along hoping that in her touching the wall it would reveal its secrets.

Except, she felt nothing.

Her hand moved through the structure as if it wasn't there. She nearly fell over because she had expected to catch herself on the wall. Half of her forearm was gone but she could still move her fingers. She kicked at the wall. Where her foot should have connected it just disappeared. *An illusion.* Her heart dropped knowing that she's seen something like this before just not of this magnitude. She stepped into the wall.

The light from the cold October day vanished. It was completely dark but she kept moving forward. After a few moments of walking with her hands out in front of her, she felt the temperature change. Outside the sun was at least keeping the air warm but suddenly her fingers were freezing. She emerged into a small space between the illusion and another wall. Her fingers could touch this one, however.

In front of her was a long row of windows that went in either direction. Asteria realized she was looking at the outside wall of a school hallway. Then it hit her like a train, the cement covered an entire school. *He is here.*

It was a stray thought, she didn't mean to think it but now that she had, it infected her mind. All of this cement must be his doing, she thought. Asteria looked down the hall as far as she could see but it seemed empty.

She stood looking at the glass, she wondered if she ought to break it or try to open it. She decided trying to open seemed a little less noisy so she went with that. She heard a latch click as she pushed it to a side then felt it move. The glass slid into the wall. She hoisted herself up the ledge then fell into the hall on her feet.

The fall was longer than she expected. Her feet slammed against the linoleum with a resounding slap. Staring at the opposite wall she read the words JUDGMENT IS COMING from a half torn poster.

"Who are you?" It was the same voice that she had just heard a little bit ago and it came from beside her. She turned to see a young Mexican boy staring her down gripping a gun in his right hand.

"I'm looking for someone, his name is Stephen-" Asteria began but the boy raised his gun to her eye level and the rest of her sentence got trapped in her throat.

[3: 47 P.M.]

The Crown

AUBREY
October 15, 1999
[11: 05 A.M.]

The lunchroom was beginning to fill with the chaos of teenagers. Aubrey was standing in line waiting for food. Michelle stood closely behind her watching everyone. The last couple of classes seemed to drag but finally, the day was half over.

"I don't know about you," Aubrey said to Michelle. "But, I could use some sleep." The mute smiled letting her know she heard her. From the other side of the room, Manny entered. A group of kids watched him and then glanced over at Aubrey.

"What do you think that was about?" she asked her friend. "Everyone at this school seems so hostile." Michelle wasn't listening. She was watching Manny.

He noticed people looking at him as he found a spot to sit. His stomach turned at the thought of food. This would be just another hour closer to being able to leave unnoticed, he thought to himself. This school had no answers for him, at least not to the questions he was asking. A girl walked from the food line directly to where he was sitting.

She had dark hair and an angry look about her. He liked it. She slipped her tan legs under the table next to him as she sat with her food. The plate held a slab of bread that wanted to be a slice of pizza and a bottle of water. He watched her for a moment.

She seemed to be radiating this sort of light from all around her. She was wearing a black dress that reminded him of a girl named Jamie. Suddenly all at once, he felt he could not remember the name and it disappeared forever. Manny closed his eyes trying to stop the escape of thoughts and when he opened them he noticed the chains along her waist. He followed them to her eyes, dark brown holding back an irritability of existing. He wondered if she knew he was even there.

"Do you need something?" he asked her, sounding more annoyed than he meant.

"You see those girls over there?" she asked, ignoring his question. He followed her glare to Aubrey and Michelle. His stomach sank.

"Yeah," he responded.

"It's disgusting," the pretty girl said, taking a sip from her water. "What's your name?"

"Manny, yours?"

"Evrona. Who are you?"

"What do you mean?"

"You just seem a little old to be in high school," she said with a shrug. "If I'm being honest I don't really care. I watched the way you defended yourself against that girl. I was close to shutting her up myself. She got lucky. I hate people like that. The ones that get lucky."

"What do you mean you were going to shut her up?" Manny asked, finding himself getting excited. He needed to change the subject. "I can handle myself." He imagined grabbing the girl by her throat until she couldn't breathe. His heart was racing.

"That stupid girl needed to show some respect," Evrona said. Manny didn't hear the words. His eyes were focusing on her neck. He stood from his chair. Something was wrong. This wasn't where he was supposed to be, he just knew it.

A sudden crashing from across the room broke Manny free from his torment. Two kids were fighting over a silver crown. It had the same light Evrona was giving off, but only for a moment. The sight of the piece of metal seemed to call to him. Evrona was already halfway across the room shouting. It was when Aubrey left the lunch line that Manny decided to get involved.

"Get off of me!" The shout came from one of the kids who held the crown. "I found it first!".

Aubrey pushed her way through the crowd catching a glimpse of Manny standing with the girl that randomly yelled at her earlier.

"It doesn't matter if you found it first; you have no idea whose it is!" the boy who was with Manny in the hall yelled. They were both on the ground wrestling and struggling to keep a grip on the crown. Aubrey stood to the side, she had been prepared to jump in and stop the fight, but it didn't seem worth it. This wasn't her problem.

"I don't care whose it is! It's mine now," The boy yelled back at Drake. The struggle only went on for a few more moments before someone pushed past Aubrey and snatched the crown from them. It was the mean girl.

"Give that back Evrona! It's not yours and I found it first!" the boy on the ground yelled up at her trying to get to his feet. The pretty girl spat on him and kicked his side before he could get up.

"There was no need for that!" Drake yelled at her but stayed on the ground. Aubrey watched as fear spread across his face.

"Shut your mouth, you disgusting little boy!" Evrona yelled down at him. She spat on him as well. "This crown is mine. I am the only one here worthy enough to wear it. Anyone who thinks differently had better come and take this from me, right now!" The lunch room was quiet. No one moved.

"What else should I have expected from all of you disgusting creatures? I am the only one worthy of this crown because unlike you I have the willpower to change and challenge. Where is your courage? Disgusting, none of you think you could take this from a little girl like me? I dare you to try." While Evrona said the last sentence her eyes had come to rest on Aubrey.

"I'll stand up for it," Aubrey said without thinking. It was like she didn't have a choice. This girl was practically challenging her. She hesitantly took a step forward into the circle.

"Will you now?" Evrona said, turning the rest of her body toward her. The dress she was wearing spun around her body wrapping around her legs. The look on her face was pure enjoyment. The rest of the room fell silent.

"I don't know why you have such a problem with other people. Honestly, it's kind of annoying. You can't just bully people for no reason. What? You're cute? Good for you. You don't just get what you want." Aubrey found herself now standing in a circle surrounded by strangers.

Evrona stood across from her. She couldn't tell whether the girl was amused or aggravated but either way she said her peace. A smile appeared on her face. It was a mask for the anger. The pretty girl grasped the crown and pleasurably set it on her head. The satisfaction that appeared on her face was vicious, ruthless even, but undoubtedly full of a fury that Aubrey could feel.

"Take the crown if you are so strong." Evrona stood still with her arms out at her sides prepared to take a hit.

Aubrey jumped at the pretty girl without thinking. In the air she only had one thought, this was a mistake. Since she was being called out, she would defend everyone from this girl. Deep down she really wanted to prove to herself she could do it. She wondered if Michelle, Manny, or Stephen were watching. Evrona wasn't expecting her to fight back. The hand that reached for the crown caught her off guard.

Instead of metal, Aubrey felt hair. She grabbed and pulled as hard as she could. A small fist reached her cheek. The crown fell to the ground. Aubrey watched as another fist approached her face. She couldn't move as it made contact. Her vision dulled. The hair between her fingers reminded her to defend herself. Again, she pulled, this time Evrona stumbled into Aubrey. Their bones collided, bruising both of them. At this point, Evrona decided to throw her hands wildly at Aubrey.

It didn't hurt that much, Aubrey thought, and with her free hand, she created a fist and threw it at Evrona's face. This was the first time Aubrey ever hit someone with a fist. Her wrist buckled as it made contact. She hoped it hurt the pretty girl just as much as it hurt her.

Suddenly, the two girls were on the ground, locked together, kicking. The blur of the crowd surrounded them. *Why was no one helping?*

Through the blur of arms and black hair, Aubrey could have sworn she could see hints of a red mist hovering over the crowd.

"Stop!" Aubrey recognized the voice. Manny was standing over them pulling on Aubrey's arm.

As the two separated, Aubrey found the crown in her hand. She raised herself to her hands and knees. Evrona watched Aubrey scramble and grabbed the crown. Then, all three of them had a hand on the piece of metal. Aubrey was hit in the stomach, taking all the fight from her. Manny let go and attempted to subdue Evrona, who now had both hands on the crown used the leverage to kick him into the crowd.

Before Aubrey knew it, the pretty girl was sitting on top of her. Through the tears and sweat, Aubrey could only see a dark shadow and it was smiling. Evrona raised the crown above her head and slammed it into Aubrey's face. Her head hit the floor.

"Hey!" someone yelled. Both Aubrey's vision and hearing blurred into a haze. She could see red. Then Evrona raised the crown above her head again, but someone stopped the pretty girl from hitting Aubrey again.

Manny pulled Evrona off Aubrey's chest. Aubrey took a deep breath but choked on her own saliva. Her face felt swollen. Evrona yelled obscenities at Manny. The fight was over.

"Do you see these people?" Evrona yelled out, throwing her arms wildly. "They're fake! I thought Manny would be strong like me, but he's just like her. Scared. What, you can't stand the sight of a predator eating prey? Pathetic. You people, in this crowd, people that would call themselves *friends* you're even worse. No one else had the guts to claim the crown. Scared of conflict? I'm sick and tired of acting like we're all friends. Does anyone else think they can take this from me?"

"Enough!" Manny yelled. His voice scared even him. He felt his heart beating in his chest. Not again, he thought. "We get it."

Evrona put the crown back on her head and spat out a collection of blood and spit. She looked right at Manny as she did it. She was tempting him. Blood was trickling down the left side of her bottom lip. Manny's heart raced. All at once he loved the sight and felt shame. It was her smile, it reminded him of someone. He looked over at Michelle.

The mute was kneeling beside Aubrey with her hand on her back. Aubrey was trying to get to her feet but her head wouldn't stop spinning and she couldn't seem to fully clear her throat. An image flashed before Manny's eyes.

He could see a girl, naked, chained against a wall somewhere in a basement. She was covered in dirt and dried blood. She was smiling at him. Beside her was another girl, he didn't recognize her but her bare back was bruised. He watched as the girl began to weep. Then he heard a scream and the vision was gone.

He was standing over Evrona with the crown in his hand. His other hand was raised dripping blood onto Evrona's black dress. She was on the ground with her arms raised to protect herself. There was a hand holding his arm from moving. He glanced back to see a tired face. It was Aubrey.

Manny pulled his arm free and threw the crown to the ground. For a moment it seemed to shine a brilliant black aura. Manny looked into the crowd to see if anyone else had seen it. Only Michelle was staring at it.

"What else was I supposed to do?" he said when he noticed the disgusted eyes on him. "Someone had to stop her. She's right about one thing. You all are weak. You have no problem letting me make the hard decisions, let me be your monster." It was pointless. He knew it. Everyone was already on Aubrey's side. Guilt and shame washed over Manny. He decided to just leave. He pushed his way through the crowd and exited out into the hall.

Aubrey knelt beside Evrona, comforting her. It was one thing for her and the pretty girl to fight, at least it was a fair fight. The way Manny hit the girl in the black dress, the smile on Manny's face, gave his pleasure away.

"I'm sorry that happened to you," Aubrey said. "No one should enjoy hurting other people. Including you." Evrona nodded while covering her face. The once strong pretty girl was crying.

"Alright people!" Drake yelled out to the crowd trying to take control of the situation. "We're done here." Most of the crowd dispersed leaving the two girls to collect themselves.

The crown remained on the floor hidden in shadows. Everyone seemed to forget that it existed. The lunchroom went back to the busy sounds of plastic trays and shouting teenagers. The crown remained.

[11: 38 A.M.]

Looking Forward

MANNY
October 15, 1999
[11: 40 A.M.]

Manny entered the front office, finding it empty. There had to be more information here about him. He spotted the cabinets in the back of the room. As he flipped through the papers, the images he saw in the cafeteria flashed before him.

"What are you looking for?" a familiar voice said coming from the door. Drake was watching him.

"You scared me," Manny responded, going back to the papers. "Something's not right about this whole situation. Why can't I remember anything? Why are all the teachers here but none of the faculty like administrators or secretaries? I have a feeling that if I can figure out more about myself maybe that'll be a clue." Student names whipped past his vision as he closed the drawer and opened the one below it.

"Have you remembered anything?" Drake said with an annoyed tone. Manny ignored it. He didn't really feel like talking about what happened just a few minutes ago.

"Nothing," he lied. "I'm sure I've been to school because I feel as old as you, but I can't remember any of it. This school isn't familiar and you don't know me so I at least know I didn't go here. Wouldn't my parents be wondering where I am? Unless they are the ones that put me here... I wish I could remember!"

"Let's try something," Drake said. "I feel like you haven't taken a moment to just stop and think since I've met you. So just stop. Take a pause and concentrate. Start from what you do remember and try working backward."

Manny slammed the drawer shut, at first he was prepared to yell, but maybe Drake was right. He found a chair and sat down. He took a breath.

"I remember a bright light and a girl," Manny said, closing his eyes. "Michelle, I remember her. I can recall only up to dragging her out of the crater near the school. She was injured. None of these images in my head make any sense. I remember orange eyes and a fog, or maybe dust... I had a friend, but I can't remember his name... it was urgent... there was a park... a parade...? There was an explosion... no... an earthquake? I don't... I can't... This is frustrating!"

The room fell silent. Drake put his hand on Manny's shoulder. "Calm down," he said in a soft voice. "Try again." Manny nodded and closed his eyes. Darkness enveloped him.

The image of the crown entered his mind. It seemed to be engulfed by black flames. He saw bright orange eyes, he could hear a girl's voice. He could remember what it was saying but couldn't hear it. She was begging him to kill someone and to be let go. Again, the image of the basement appeared before him. Her voice was muffled and contained in a thick gray fog. The closer he seemed to get to the scene the harder it was to hear. There was blood dripping from his hands.

He watched himself raise his hand to a girl's face smearing the liquid across her face then down her chest. She was still smiling. He heard himself ask her if he could trust her. She nodded aggressively. Doubt filled his heart as she began to speak again. Only one word slipped through the fog.

"Mikal."

"Who's that?" Drake asked.

"I don't know," Manny responded. He shook the vision from his mind.

"Did you remember anything?" the young boy asked eagerly.

"No." A lie. Manny glanced over at the computer atop the secretary's desk, it looked new. He didn't remember everything, but he remembered enough. Unfortunately, there were now more questions than answers. He needed to find Michelle. She knew more than him. He could feel it.

"I don't belong here," Manny said standing up. At the same time, the bell rang for class to start.

"What are you going to do?" Drake asked, making his way to the door.

"I'm leaving," Manny said. "But, first I've got to finish something."

The two young men exited the office. They found the hall crowded. Manny walked with Drake looking for Michelle.

"This is my class," the boy said to Manny. "Good luck with everything." Drake entered the classroom leaving him alone in an empty hall. Manny ran back to the last place he saw Michelle, the lunchroom. He found the doors and threw them open. The room was empty except for a boy sitting at one of the tables. Skipping class, Manny thought to himself.

"Hey," Manny yelled out to him. "Did you see where those two new girls went?"

The kid ignored Manny as he took a drink from a water bottle. Angered, Manny went up to him and grabbed his shoulder. "Did you hear me?"

"I heard you," the kid lazily replied, turning his head. Manny watched as the kid seemed to shine just as the crown had. The light faded as Manny locked eyes. They were silver.

Aubrey walked down the windowed hallway. She was alone as she stared out at the crater, which was now clearly visible in the afternoon sunlight. The bell for lunch to end rang around her. Five minutes before the next class was to start. That was enough time to go out there and check out the crater, she thought to herself.

It was colder out than it had been in the last couple of days. Aubrey could remember the morning and how cold it had been. The clothes she was wearing didn't match the weather. This is what was in her mind as she approached the crater's rim. The scene now looked welcoming. The grass all around rested in the afternoon air. Behind the crater, tall trees loomed as if attempting to peer inside to see the bottom. Aubrey mimicked the posture as she stepped onto the rim.

Dirt lined the walls, along with grass and reddish clay that seemed to coat most of the walls of the crater. At the bottom, there was nothing but a puddle of water from the morning dew buildup. Aubrey was expecting something more than an empty crater and some creepy trees. She wanted answers to questions she hadn't even formulated yet. They are all rooted in one story that was untold. Michelle was mute and Manny couldn't remember anything.

Aubrey thought of a new question, what could have happened to cause one person who was involved to go mute and the other to lose their memory? She wondered if Michelle was mute before her injury. She also considered the possibility of Manny having memory problems before the incident. These factors could indicate that there was no incident terribly horrific and that the two just happened to come across each other at that moment in time when Michelle was injured.

This couldn't be it; she thought to herself, something bad happened to Michelle. The injuries on her chest proved it but what was it? *Manny could be lying.*

Aubrey's breath stopped short at that thought. Her vision blurred and she felt gross, trapped even. If Manny was lying then she could have just let a relentless murderer into her new school and set him loose on the innocent students. *Mostly innocent.* It would explain why he disappeared after they brought Michelle to the nurse's office. It wouldn't explain why Manny took an interest in the affairs and happenings back in the lunchroom or why he was enrolled as a new student on the same day she was, or would it?

That could be the reason he left, she thought, to mark himself down in a few classes so he could create an alibi for himself amongst the other students. Aubrey didn't want to think about this anymore. Earlier when she approached the crater, the Mexican boy had called for help first before he even knew she was there. Would someone attempting murder draw attention to himself? This thought brought her nerves down just a tad but he could have heard her coming and thought to make it seem like he was trying to help instead of trying to do harm. The injuries that Michelle had couldn't be from someone's bare hands, it didn't seem that way anyways. Nothing added up.

The only logical explanation she had was that Michelle got the injuries and *then* Manny found her there then lost his memory, but that didn't seem to add up either because it was too coincidental and would seem to rely on too many factors. She didn't want to think about this anymore. What could have happened to Manny for him to lose his memory?

With fear in her mind, she turned to leave and came face to face with Michelle.

"Hi," Aubrey said weakly. She didn't know how long Michelle was behind her. The girl looked into her eyes then to the crater then back to her eyes. Aubrey wanted her to say something so she could not stand there in awkward silence. Michelle walked over to the crater and knelt down to see inside.

The trees seemed to mimic her this time. Aubrey thought of the way she was carrying herself. It was like she just buried a lover. Tears formed around Michelle's eyes.

"Are you okay?" Aubrey asked, stepping towards her. She felt dumb though, she knew the girl couldn't talk. The pain she was feeling was hers alone to endure. Aubrey watched Michelle as she looked up into the sky. It looked like she was praying but religion didn't seem to suit the girl.

"Do you even know where you are?" Again like the question before she felt dumb. At least this one was a yes or no question.

Michelle took her attention back down from the sky and shook her head. Her eyes were just as radiant as they were this morning. The smile on her face could not hide the pain in her eyes. Michelle wiped the tears away. The smile shouldn't exist. Aubrey hoped the girl was finding happiness in unspoken stories of memories she did not share.

Aubrey's mind went back to the morning, she could see Michelle sprawled about at the bottom of the crater painted with blood and dust like a fallen angel.

The mute pulled on Aubrey's arm pulling her back to reality. The girl pulled out her schedule and pushed it again into Aubrey's face. Then used it to point down into the hole. Aubrey could see nothing. Michelle walked around the crater to the trees on the other side. Aubrey walked to the edge of the crater. Between them was a hole with no explanation. Michelle pointed at the hole then pointed at herself. She was trying to say something but Aubrey didn't understand.

When Michelle jumped into the crater Aubrey wasn't ready for it.

She watched the oversized t-shirt flutter as if trying to grasp onto something behind Michelle. Her feet hit the walls allowing her to slide down, all the way to the bottom. The size of the crater hadn't been considered until she witnessed this. It was at least as deep as two of her height, maybe more and there was the girl, with a smile on her face standing at the bottom. She was looking around for something, Aubrey noticed.

"What are you looking for?" Aubrey shouted down, she asked because she was curious but the fact that she was mute came back into her head. She felt dumb, if she was going to be talking to this girl and seeing her around school she would have to remember that she was mute. Michelle reached down into the dirt and pulled from it a long black feather. It was nearly the size of Michelle's forearm.

The girl stood for a moment staring at it. Her eyes were looking at the feather like it was a long lost lover. She put it against her chest and held it tightly. Something about the object made the girl so happy she was on the verge of tears. With the feather in hand, the girl began to exit the crater.

Aubrey helped the girl out of the hole as a breeze picked up sending a chill down her back. This girl confused her, but she was happy that Michelle was happy. They walked back to the school. As they made their way back to the building she felt someone was watching them. She turned around looking back at the trees.

They blocked the sun casting shadows onto the forest floor. Anyone could be hiding out there. Aubrey watched for a moment. The forest seemed to breathe as another gust of wind rushed by. The string of cold reached her busted lip. Maybe it was nothing, she thought to herself.

The two girls entered the building and walked down to their class. Back inside her cold skin welcomed the heat. The halls were scarce of students as everyone entered their classes. The pair soon found themselves at the threshold of their next period. The room was filled with students but no teacher. On the board was a large number, the same as the one outside on the door. They found seats near the front and waited. A few minutes passed and the bell chimed for the start of class.

Still no teacher.

Aubrey looked around at the rest of the room. Everyone seemed to be just as confused as her.

"I wonder if it's another sub," she heard someone say.

"What do you mean another sub?" she asked the kid. He looked to Aubrey.

"Well," he replied. "All the classes I've had today have had substitute teachers." Aubrey felt her heart drop. "Now that I think about it none of the adults I've seen today looked familiar."

"That doesn't seem strange to you?" Aubrey yelled, she didn't mean to. She stood and ran to the door. She turned the handle and pulled but it didn't move. A girl screamed and a shadow was cast over the windows like a slow moving fire. Aubrey looked at Michelle. The mute hadn't noticed, she was looking down at her feather.

The speaker above beeped as the same voice that spoke that morning began to talk.

Manny entered a quiet hall feeling unsure. The conversation he just had left a bad taste in his mouth. He felt the weight of responsibility on his shoulders. It competed with the new weight he felt in his pocket. As the kid said, he had two options. The door on his right had an exit sign above it and the door on his left was the same one Drake went through earlier.

This was his choice. He could leave, or partake.

"If you leave," the boy had said. "I'm guessing you might live a full life, but that would be a waste. If you stay, if you play, you can help me." The boy's tongue was just as silver as his eyes. "If you succeed you will inherit fire."

Manny wasn't sure what he meant by that but felt something move within him. He didn't have a choice. *Did he ever?*

Manny took to the left and approached the door to the classroom. He could hear someone talking behind the door. He entered the room, as the door shut behind him he heard the lock engage with a resounding thud. He made his choice. Several minutes later, the windows darkened as the speaker above once again beeped preparing to dispel another announcement.

Manny scanned the room wondering who he had to work with, other than Drake. In the back Evrona sat alone, staring at him with fierce eyes.

"Hello, again," the voice said, creeping through the drone of static. "If I haven't met you yet, my name is Stephen Kenward. Today has been a day of trials for some and discovery for others. My friends and I took the beginning of the day as an opportunity to remind you of some fundamentals of ethics and existence. I hoped that this would give you the tools necessary to participate in my experiment.

"I want you to know. I used to be a student here. Sure, that was a few years ago, but it seemed none of you remembered me. That's fine I suppose. Probably for the best. I remembered you though. I remember the torturous nature of high school. Rather trivial, in my opinion. I figured this would be the best place to perform our tests. The outcome of which would determine everything.

"You see, we have found ourselves staring down the end of the world. I know, that's a lot to take in, but there is no need to be afraid, because I've seen it. I've seen how it all ends. I've seen how I can stop it.

"And, I can stop it.

"The issue I have is whether or not I should. After all, my whole life has been nothing but suffering from my parents, my friends, even the teachers and faculty that used to work in this very building. I've seen innocent people hurt and mangled and tortured by the very people sworn to protect them. I have to believe that what I've seen is only a small part of the picture. Sure, mine is painted with blood but there has to be good in this world. Justice? Maybe not, but at the very least people will stand up and take the pain for others. Right? There has to be. Anyways, that is what we are all here to prove today.

"It started with the crown. That was the first test. I figured if everyone just ignored it and no one tried to claim it for themselves then the world must be worth saving and I'll go out there and save everyone.

"You failed.

"Not only did someone try to claim it, but you all also fought over it. If you failed that test, that single simple test then I'd be forced to carry out multiple tests. You may have noticed the world outside is blocked off. We are all trapped here together. Each classroom will be tested individually. I'm not sure if this will clear things up for me, but I really, really hope it does. Think of it this way, the fate of the world now rests on all of our shoulders. We can get through this, can't we?

"Not only will each room be tested, but we have also rigged all the rooms to slowly fill with water. We don't have time to spare. Let's say, one hour. In one hour if you don't complete your test we will not unlock the door.

"So, let's begin."

[12: 07 P.M.]

Crimson Origins

MANNY
April 3, 2011
[4: 21 A.M.]

It was raining when Manny found himself out again, walking the streets of the sleeping city wishing he was home. Of course, this would be the last time he kept reminding himself. Water dripped into his gloves. The tips of his fingers couldn't even feel the fabric anymore. In the dark, the lights from the streetlamps and windows seemed to dance on the walls casting shadows back and forth. Tonight he felt like a shadow.

The buildings towered over him making him feel small, unimportant, and maybe a little ashamed for what he was about to do. He had to do this though, every night he put it off resulting in less and less sleep. With only two hours remaining before sunrise Manny decided it was time.

The streets seemed too loud for the hour. Cars rushed beside him splashing water into the gutters, merchants shouted at people on the street, and garbage trucks moved through alleys disturbing cats as they slept. Manny stood in front of an apartment building looking at the window he'd looked out of so many times. Ascending the steps to press the doorbell felt like an eternity.

The sound of the buzzer sent shivers up his arms. He waited. The world seemed to fall silent and still. Then her voice echoed off the glass door in front of him. Somehow it seemed to awaken the rain as the wind picked up.

"Hello?" a tired voice answered. *The voice I should hear every morning,* he thought to himself.

"Hey, it's me," he responded, his voice soft from shame. The door buzzed and Manny made his way into the building. He found his way to the elevator and began his ascent. Standing still for so long reminded him of the pain in his leg. The elevator dinged and Manny left the puddle he made for someone else to deal with.

The door to her room was already open. She was standing there waiting for him. Her hair was messy from the sleep he interrupted. The makeup from the night before was still there, half cleaned off her face. She was wearing pajamas, a shirt that was just a little too small for her chest without a bra, and a pair of tattered boxers.

"What do you want?" she asked through yawns. Her arms were crossed. She looked cold. "Do you know what time it is?"

"I know, I know," he said, trying to calm himself down. "Something happened. Mikal, he…" he purposefully let his voice trail off. "There was an accident."

The shock woke her up.

"What the hell do you mean something happened?" she yelled, running back into the apartment. Manny took a long look at the room. It was messy but not dirty. To his right, the kitchen had a few dishes piled to the side of the sink, and the small round dining table was littered with bills and ads from the mail. On the other side of the room sat a couch with a modest T.V. in front of it.

"He was playing a show just down the street! I didn't hear anything." Her voice was shaking as she tied her shoes. "Why didn't you just call me? Were you with him?" Manny didn't respond, he took a step into the room closing the door behind him. She grabbed her coat and ran up to the door finding Manny blocking the exit.

"Come on man! Move." She pushed against his chest but he didn't budge. His heart was racing. The panic in her heart lowered her defenses. He reached up to her neck slipping his fingertips past her chest. She recoiled with a face of disgust. Then he grabbed her throat. The rain in his gloves splashed back up his sleeve. She pulled away, the water allowed the glove to move with her body but he stepped into the motion.

The weight of their bodies put a dent into the drywall. She threw a closed fist at his head but it slipped against his wet hair with her other hand she was grabbing at anything she could. She found a decorative geode on the kitchen counter but it was too late. Her eyes rolled to the back of her head as she gasped for air. Manny released his grip. She wouldn't die tonight. The rock fell from her hand hitting the carpet.

She fell to her hands and knees, coughing. Manny grabbed the geode from the ground and hit her in the back of the head. Her body hit the ground with a solid thud.

Manny took a moment to examine his work. The broken wall, the blood on the floor mixing with rainwater, and somehow all the random junk on the counters had been knocked off. Not too bad, he thought to himself. Of course, it could've been better.

The girl on the ground was *his*, almost.

He took some time tying her up with a rope he had concealed under his jacket. Then he cleaned up the room and went to find her a piece of paper and a pen. The wall he would have to deal with later. He had time, most people wouldn't break down doors looking for people until a day or two after being missing. No writing utensils could be found in the living room. His only option was to check her bedroom.

This room was new to him, of course, he'd seen glimpses of it when they hung out but this was the first time he could be in there free to explore. An opportunity he did not want to waste. The bed was dressed with a black sheet and a gray comforter. It looked like she left it so she could slip back in without missing a moment of sleep. He made his way to the nightstand and grabbed her phone.

It vibrated in his hand and illuminated his face. On the screen was a message from Mikal, their friend, his *best* friend. The text talked of his show, how well it went, and how he wished she would've been there. Manny was sure she felt the same way now. He collected the phone in his pocket and made his way to the dresser.

He opened each drawer and moved the contents that lay on top. Most people hide their secrets at the bottom of sock drawers. Of course, at the bottom of her underwear drawer, he found a small box wrapped in silk. It wasn't much bigger than the phone, so he put it in the same pocket.

There was a desk opposite the dresser with an open laptop. Manny went to it and pressed the spacebar. It lit up requesting a password. He would need to get this later. From the other room, he heard something hit the ground. Fortunately, on the desk was a notebook and pen. He grabbed them then returned to his new possession.

"Don't make this harder on yourself than it has to be," he said to her as he entered the room. She was squirming, trying to break free of her restraints.

"Why are you doing this?" she asked. To Manny's surprise, there was more anger in her voice than there was fear. "What do you want?"

"I want what's mine." His voice was soft. He knelt down beside her and put his bare palm on the skin distending from her top. "You belong to me now."

She laughed.

Manny made a fist with his hand that held her flesh pulling it hard. "What's so funny?" he yelled to her.

"Is this about Mikal?" she said with fury in her voice. "You're jealous? I knew you were competitive but this is ridiculous. You couldn't just *win* my love? Make me cheat on him? You must have a tiny dick to have to resort to this. Kidnapping me?" She laughed again.

He let go of her. He could feel her skin under his fingernails. In the kitchen, he could see where she kept her tools like hammers, screwdrivers, and duct tape. Before that, he went back into the bedroom and grabbed a dirty sock off the ground. If she was going to act this way, then he was going to treat her the same.

Back in the kitchen, he threw the cabinet doors open and grabbed the tape. She was still laughing and he wanted her to shut up. He put his body on top of hers and pushed the sock in her mouth. She tried biting his hand but she missed, and good because that would be another mess he'd have to clean up. Then came the tape. He wrapped it around her head making sure to cover her mouth.

"This could've gone so much smoother," he said when his work was done. "I was going to let you write a letter to Mikal saying your final goodbye, but no!" Out of breath, Manny sat on the floor beside his prize. In this moment of silence, he felt alone again. The guilt found its way back to his heart.

"I thought I could go the rest of my life without doing this again," he said to her, defeated. "I can still see the look in her eyes when me and my brothers broke the door in. This was about a year ago when I was deployed. We were looking for some man who knew something about some bombs or something. We were good soldiers. That father pulled a gun to protect his wife and daughter, like an idiot. Soon the whole family was grouped in a corner trying to protect their dad. It was a mess.

"I was forced to take action. Our job was to bring that man back to a small base we'd made just a couple of blocks away. Whatever. I hit the daughter with my gun. I wasn't a murderer. None of us wanted to be, anyways. The crack of her skull against my stock. The most amazing sound I'd ever heard.

"And, the blood. Through the sand and musk, you could smell it.

"It was when she looked at me. The shock on her face. The way the blood ran from her nose down to her rags of a shirt. She was beautiful. That night I lay in the barracks and her face was all I could see when I closed my eyes. The way the sun reflected off the red in her hair and on her chest."

"I had to go back, and I did.

"Under the cover of night, I went back to that home. They had put up a blanket or something to cover the door, we had broken the damn door in half. I stood in the house if you could call it that. It was literally just one room with a kitchen on one side, a table in the middle, and a couple of beds on the other side.

"For too long, I stood over her while she slept. Someone had patched her up. Who would ruin such a beauty? I took my knife and raised it over her chest. I don't know what I enjoyed more, stabbing her or watching the blood pour out."

Manny noticed the girl beside him was sobbing. Where was her strength, he wondered. *Being soaked up by carpet.*

"Of course," he continued. "I'm human. When she died, nothing, not her painted body, not the taste of her blood, not even feeling my fingers gliding through the warm liquid against her soft skin could make me feel the same pleasure as when she was alive and I was doing the same things."

"I felt bad. I'm not a monster. There before me lying on the bed was a dead girl. Plain and simple and I was responsible. I vowed then and there, *if* I ever did this again, I would not kill."

"That night, however, after the vows were made and the girl was slain. The mother woke up. She shot me in my leg and I slit her throat. That was self-defense, completely different."

Manny hit his leg. The pain traveled all the way to the back of his head.

"I thought I could never do this again. A couple of months ago I hired a whore and slaughtered her in her home. I made the killing last a week. I thought after that I got it all out of my system, but as the nights passed that girl's face appeared in my dreams. Then whenever I closed my eyes."

"So, here we are. Mikal doesn't deserve you. I will take care of you."

Light filled the room from the window on the east side of the building. The red water reflected the light off the ground and onto the wall. Manny sat beside Holly far longer than he anticipated. This was the first time he'd ever told that story. She was still sobbing when Manny spread his fingers into the pool of blood that was gathering behind her head. The warmth spread over his hand in a tangle of hair and crimson. He tightened his grip. *This is why I am alive.*

"You are mine."

[8:17 A.M.]

Room 213

AUBREY
October 15, 1999
[12: 10 P.M.]

"Room two thirteen, among you, there is one of my people. If you can figure out who it is, we unlock the door. You already know what happens when the time is up. When you think you have the right person, write their name in chalk on the board." Stephen continued with the remaining rooms but Aubrey couldn't hear it anymore. She was waiting impatiently to hear their task. Now they have it.

Aubrey looked around the room. She was standing near the chalkboard at the desk that was closest to the door. It stood as a sealed barrier between them and freedom. Beside her was the teacher's desk. It sat lonely and ignored at the front of the room. Resting on the top were some papers and trinkets, even a picture of a middle-aged woman in her wedding dress. Nothing useful. Past was a cabinet that reached the ceiling and an obelisk in the corner. She guessed it had books and paper and other school supplies. It stood along a long wall lined with windows. The lights reflected off of them, nearly creating a mirror where all her classmates were scrambling like blurred insects when it started to rain. The room itself consisted of twenty or so desks that were once in four by five lines but now were being pushed aside. There were ten other students in the room. Most of them were gathered in their friend groups, Aubrey figured. Except for one kid who was staring out the window at the wall that had formed before their eyes. They were too focused on discussing what just happened. This was all a shock for Aubrey, but the events from this morning seemed to have prepared her mind for this test. She felt calm. Ready.

From the ceiling, water started trickling in through the spaces between the foam panels and slivers of plastic. It felt like rain. The splattering water echoed from the walls.

Michelle grabbed Aubrey's arm to get her attention. She looked back and watched as the scared tortured soul pointed to herself.

"It's you?" Aubrey asked, keeping her voice so quiet there was no way Michelle even heard her. She grabbed Michelle's hand and pulled it down. *It couldn't be possible.* She was with her all day. Aubrey turned around to make sure no one had seen Michelle claim the role.

"What is happening?" one of the kids yelled.

"Who was that?" another asked.

"Can you try opening the door?" one of the girls closest to Aubrey asked. She grabbed the metal and twisted. The knob wouldn't turn. She expected that. The realization that they were trapped inside a room that was filling with water seemed to set into the crowd. Some screamed. Some got angry. Others started crying. Aubrey weighed her options.

"Everyone, please," she finally said, taking way too long thinking about Michelle's claim. "We don't have time to cry or scream. Let's start trying to figure this out."

She got their attention, but it wasn't enough.

"Why should we listen to you?" the same girl that asked Aubrey to try the door asked. "I don't even know you. Why should I play this game? Why is he even doing this?" All valid questions, but the water gathering at their feet made Aubrey feel they were focused on the wrong thing.

"That's actually a good point," Aubrey said, finding some use in the girl's words. "I don't know any of you, and none of you know me, or Michelle for that matter. Maybe we start by introducing ourselves and seeing if anyone's story sounds off."

For too long the only sound in the room was the drops hitting the inch of water that was now rising above their shoes.

"Fine," Aubrey said, reaching into her pocket. "My name is Aubrey Hammond. I'm sixteen. I just recently moved here because my parents are getting a divorce. This is my schedule that I got today in the front office. Does anyone else want to introduce themselves?"

"I guess I can," one of the girls responded. "My name is Samantha, you can call me Sam. I've lived here my whole life along with Dustin, over there, and my neighbor, Emily, she lives on my street and Julie who lives the other way." As Sam spoke the other's names she pointed to them. "I've got a little brother and an older sister who moved away. Should I say something about my parents?" She looked to Dustin, who shrugged.

"Good," Aubrey interrupted. "So, we can immediately rule you four out. See? This won't be that hard. We've just got to get through this with clear heads." Aubrey scanned the room, there were six left.

"I've seen most everyone in this room around school before, except you two," one of the guys who had been sitting in the back spoke up. He gestured to Aubrey and Michelle. "And, that guy that's still sitting by the window acting like he's too cool for this."

Michelle attempted to walk past Aubrey, but she moved in her way. As she did she noticed the water was now high enough to fill her shoes.

"Ok," she spoke up quickly. "Well, hi, I'm Aubrey and this is Michelle. We were both new students today. What are your guys' names?" She couldn't let Michelle try to say she was the one they were looking for. She was still trying to figure out what Michelle meant by it. There had to be another reason for her to say she was the one.

"I'm Ben," the loudest one responded. He sounded frustrated. "These are my boys, Chris and Josh. Don't change the subject. Has anyone ever seen that kid before?" His voice reverberated off the windows as he shouted. He was pointing to the kid next to the window. The rest of the kids in the room shook their heads. Aubrey had a bad feeling about this.

The kid was staring out the window at the cement wall. Through his oversized glasses, his eyes were unblinking. He was just a scared scrawny kid in shock. This Ben guy was going to make a mistake. As soon as the thought formulated in her mind Ben made his way to the kid. He grabbed his shaggy brown hair and pulled to get his attention.

"What's your name?" Ben yelled at him. A part of Aubrey wanted to go pull Ben off the kid but to do that she would leave Michelle unprotected.

"Get off me!" the kid screamed. His voice pierced their ears. "We're all gonna die!" This is exactly what Aubrey didn't want. She yelled across the room words that went unheard. She watched as the two other boys that were sitting with Ben sloshed through the water toward the kid.

"Calm down," he said back to Aubrey. "I'm not going to hurt him. I'm not a psychopath like you or Evrona or that other Mexican guy. I saw you guys at lunch." He turned his attention to the kid. "Right? You're going to tell me your name." He pushed his head away, letting go of his hair.

"I'm not telling you my name," he said quietly. "I've literally gone to school with all of you for the last two years. How do you not know my name?" The other kids in the room looked embarrassed for a moment.

"That's Nick, you idiots," one of the remaining unnamed students said. "And don't lie, if you were alone or if there was someone in here you wanted to impress, you'd bully him, like you guys always do." Michelle moved closer to Aubrey. She felt water soak through her pants touching her knees.

"That's not true!" Ben defended himself.

"Just leave him alone," one of the other unnamed students said. Aubrey took their appearance in. They looked like they were groupies for some punk band. Their hair was black and long and they both wore black shirts and pants with chains. "We're Mercy and Kim, in case some of you forgot."

"Okay," Aubrey said, trying to take control of the situation again. "So, we've got you three who are fine. Then the four boys over there. They're safe. You two. Can anyone say they've seen you well before today?" Sam chimed in saying she'd always seen them around school but never really talked to them. "Good. So you two are fine. Remember, basically as long as one person can vouch for you that you have always gone to school here then we can consider you safe. We're only looking for a single person that shouldn't be here. The last person who doesn't have someone speak about them has also been the quietest."

The room's attention went to a boy who was standing in the corner furthest from the windows and Aubrey. The whole time he hadn't said anything. His golden hair was turning dark from the water. He was wearing a black sweatshirt and jeans. Even as their eyes went to him he chose to stay quiet.

"I didn't even notice him until now," Ben said mostly to his two friends. "He looks familiar but I can't remember ever seeing him. Do you guys recognize him?" The group of boys moved through the water to the kid. The water was to their thighs making it harder to lift their legs.

"Don't touch me," the boy said to them. His voice was sharp and rough. "This is ridiculous. I'm not playing this game."

The group of boys were standing beside the boy but they didn't get too close. They were looking at each other trying to convince at least one of themselves to approach him. No one had the courage. It occurred to Aubrey that they may not have as much time as they thought. Would the chalk write on a wet board? She wasn't sure.

"Guys!" Aubrey said, trying to get their attention. They all ignored her. Desks began to lift from the ground and float around in the water. Aubrey trudged through the waist high water to the blackboard and grabbed all the chalk. She had to make sure it didn't get wet.

"Just tell us your name," Sam yelled from the middle of the room. All the kids were focused on the kid in the corner. Aubrey had no clue if he was the imposter or not. She didn't know any of these kids before this class. She'd leave it to them to figure out. She felt stuck.

If she gave up Michelle, they would all live, easy enough, but if they all lived what would they do to them? Sure, now they are acting civil enough, but who's to say this is the last test? Would it be worth it to just let everyone, including herself, drown in this room? There would be consequences if they find out Michelle is an imposter *and* that Aubrey hid that from them.

Aubrey's best bet was one of the other classrooms would pass their test and then open the doors to the other classrooms. *Someone would think of that, right?* She looked back over to the kids arguing. She had her doubts.

"No one can say they've ever seen you before!" Chris yelled from behind Ben. "If you just tell us your name it might make us remember." The kids were forming a circle around the reluctant teenager. His face was half hidden in shadows from the hood of his sweatshirt. The water was now at their stomachs, making it hard to stand in one place as everyone else moved around.

Aubrey went for the door. She started knocking and screaming for anyone to hear. "We are in here!" she shouted. For all she knew the world outside this room was gone forever.

"It could be any three of you!" Sam yelled to no one in particular.

"Who?" Aubrey asked. Her voice sounded eerie as it echoed in the shrinking room.

"You two near the door and that kid in the corner," Sam said, making her way to Aubrey. "I've never seen either of you two before today, but like Ben said, that kid looks familiar so he's safer than either of you." The crowd took their attention away from the kid hiding under his hood.

"Hey, guys," Aubrey pleaded. "I know it's not me."

"So, it could be her?" the girl that claimed to be Mercy asked the question. She was pointing to Michelle. Aubrey felt a hand grab her arm.

"Look, no, it's neither of us." Aubrey's voice was shaking. The room was shrinking and the water was making her feel light. The sound of rain falling into a pool echoed in her head.

"Well, it has to be somebody!" This voice seemed to come from the water itself. Aubrey's vision blurred. Her chest felt heavy. Then it all made sense.

"Wait," Aubrey said, regaining her senses. "This is the same test."

"What do you mean?" Sam asked her, the anger in her voice subsiding.

"This is the same test!" Aubrey shouted. "We have to do nothing! This is Stephen's whole point, right? He wants to see if when our backs are put against the wall, will we act like animals and tear each other apart, or will we stand together, united? If we put anyone's name on that board we are wrong. Just like with the crown, our pride, our selfish behavior, cannot be what determines who we sacrifice."

The kids all took a moment to think this over. The water had gathered to their chests now. For the shorter members of the group, it was to their chins. Aubrey was holding her hand full of chalk just outside of the water.

"If I'm right," she continued. "And we write a name on the board, we lose. If I'm wrong and we write a random name on the board because obviously, no one is going to confess we have a one in ten chance of being right. So, we either go with my idea which is fifty-fifty or one in ten."

In the room next door, muffled screams soaked through the walls. The fear set in. They could die here, Aubrey thought to herself as she was lifted onto the tips of her toes. The board had just a foot outside of the water, within the next few minutes they had to make a choice.

The two girls that were dressed the same climbed on top of desks pushing them to the floor. This way they would have more time. The kid that was acting like none of this was a big deal followed suit. Aubrey paddled her way to the teacher's desk making sure to keep her arm outside the water. Michelle followed. All the students were now standing on desks.

"I don't know!" Ben yelled out, breaking the silence. His voice was much louder in the bit of air that separated the water from the ceiling.

"What if you're wrong?" Sam asked her, spitting water out of her mouth.

"If I'm wrong…" Aubrey thought about it. Before she could finish her sentence Michelle reached for the chalk in her hand. "What are you doing?" Aubrey yelled at her. The two girls struggled but eventually, Aubrey lost her footing and fell into the water. Her hands let go of the chalk as she tried to stop the fall. The pieces floated to the surface.

The kid that refused to play took the opportunity to jump for a piece. Michelle searched the surface finding a piece closest to her. She scooped it out trying to dry it as best she could then leaned from the desk to the wall. Only a few inches of space was left on the board. All the girls in the room screamed as they watched Michelle suddenly plunge into the water just as her hand hit the board. Aubrey was underneath and pulling on her legs. Finding a piece teetering near a board eraser, the nameless kid swam to the front of the class. Ben decided it best to try to escape. He swam to the windows in the class and tried to open them. His hand fumbled at a latch that moved easy. Through the window he could see there was space that the water could escape and fill, giving them more time, or might allow them to get out. Determined, he pulled the window. It refused to move.

He took a deep breath and went under to inspect the glass. In the water, he saw Aubrey and Michelle fighting for the chalk in Michelle's hand. They looked like mermaids dancing wildly. His fingers traced the window and found some type of adhesive filling the cracks. Frustrated, he kicked the window. It was pointless. Through the water, those submerged heard the soft thuds of his foot against the solid glass.

Aubrey found herself being kicked in the face. She wasn't sure if it was Michelle's boot or the other kid that had finally made his way to the board. Her grip on Michelle's hand released as she put her hands to her face. She needed air. Her vision was blurry, but she kicked her legs and her head rose from the water. She was expecting more room but there was less than a foot of air left in the room. The other kids in the room were struggling to stay afloat. The girls were screaming.

At the board, Michelle and the kid were trying to make the chalk work but everything was too saturated. The pressure from their hand to the board disintegrated the chalk into mush. Everyone was talking at the same time, throwing angry words back and forth. It mixed all together sounding like a loud drone through the patter from the raining ceiling.

They could all see the air they had left. After exchanging fearful glances, all at once, the kids in the room attempted to take the deepest breath they could muster.

The water reached the ceiling.

This was a new world. There was no sound, just a blue blur of eventual corpses floating together.

Underwater Aubrey could see Ben and his friends were punching and kicking the glass. It was lined with metal wire making it shatterproof. They were just wasting their energy. The water in front of Aubrey turned red. She was bleeding from her nose. The two girls that wore the same clothes were holding hands but already Aubrey could see they were struggling. The bigger girl needed air. She attempted to breathe.

They all watched her drown.

The girl's body shook and she began hitting her friend. But, what could she do? They stared at each other until her body stopped moving. If her friend was crying, they couldn't tell.

Aubrey felt something hit her. She looked over to see an angry Michelle glaring at her. If Aubrey could talk she would defend herself. This wasn't her fault. She didn't fill the room with water. She didn't make the girl fat. She didn't kill her. The look in Michelle's eyes told her differently. Muffled screams fell onto Aubrey.

The girl named Emily was beginning to struggle now too. Aubrey felt a pit open up inside of her. She was responsible. Then she felt herself feel the need to breathe. She pulled all her concentration together trying to hold off the reflex of inhaling as long as she could.

At the same time Aubrey took a breath, she felt a pull on her left. The room slid outside of her view and it blurred into a door frame and then the hallway. Air hit her body while she began to cough up the little water she had begun to swallow. Her body slammed against the growing pile of students.

One after the other the remainder of the water spilled out along with the teenagers, alive and dead. Aubrey's mind was on the door. She ignored the pain in her chest as she crawled over to it.

"We gotta close the door."

Aubrey was thinking of the long game. If someone had gone through the trouble of locking them in suicide rooms they probably also trapped them inside the whole building. She couldn't risk the school becoming a tomb filled with water.

She grabbed the door and pushed it shut. There was rubber along the edge creating a seal stopping the water from escaping. Aubrey rested against the wooden door finally able to catch her breath.

"You guys passed?" The voice was familiar. Aubrey looked around, finding Manny, Evrona, and a number of other kids standing around them.

[1: 02 P.M]

Forest of Red Bones

MANNY
June 7, 2012
[11: 42 P.M.]

Strangers danced in the middle of the room while the band played their ballad. The stage was lit with soft blue lights that jumped with life, illuminating the faces and movements of each musician. Mikal stood in the center, bass in hand, singing soft words. His eyes were closed letting his voice carry his emotions with every heavy breath. On either side of him, a guitarist played lone droning notes that made the listener feel like they were floating. To his back, a drummer, hitting the cymbals and snares as if they would shatter if hit hard enough. Manny was sitting far behind the crowd.

When the light hit Manny's face he was sure the whole room could see his guilt. His eyes were not on the band but on Mikal's new girlfriend. He watched as the light turned red and focused on the ceiling. Then slowly they fell back down to the crowd, like a red wave washing over everyone. The light reached her face, she was smiling. The light wasn't enough.

At this point, Manny was helping Mikal's career. The song they were playing had reached the local radio and it was about his ex-girlfriend. Heartbreak hurts worse when the girl just up and leaves. No word, no note, nothing. Relationships typically ended for good reason, but for Mikal, he was abandoned. Manny made sure to comfort his best friend in his suffering. He wondered if it made his new girl uncomfortable hearing him sing so passionately about a past lover. If the song bothered her, she would never say.

The lovestruck girl sat there, her curly dark brown hair rested on her shoulders with her auburn eyes locked on Mikal. The smile on her face could tempt any man, not in the same way it did Manny. Most men would see the straight teeth behind her full plump lips, but he wanted to see what she looked like with a mouthful of blood as it dripped from the tiny creases on either side.

Tonight she was dressed for Mikal's eyes. She wore a black shirt that revealed more of her chest than most girls dared and a tiny sliver of empty space separated her top from her modest red skirt. Every bit of skin Manny could see made his heart stir.

The song was coming to an end as Mikal's voice turned to sorrow then frustration. He was speaking to love as if it was something to be cherished even in its absence. The ending was a vow to belong to each other even if it killed you. Manny thought this was funny because love was not some temptress that someone only flirts with and then it gleefully runs away. Love had to be captured and then kept safe. If Mikal knew this, maybe tonight would play out differently.

"Isn't he amazing!" the girl beside him shouted without giving him a look. The crowd erupted well before the final notes played. This was their last song for the night. Another band entered the stage pushing Mikal and his group off, acting like they mattered more than they really did. In truth, Manny really admired Mikal.

"Thank you guys for coming out!" Mikal shouted over the bass of the new band as he approached their table. He was a shorter guy with messy light brown hair and no real muscle to be seen on his body, except for his hands. His hands were strong but if all you'd ever seen of him was his face you wouldn't guess it. His blue eyes were comforting and he wore a smile you could confide in. When you were around Mikal, you felt like you could accomplish anything.

Manny tried to look away from his soon to be prize while Mikal put his hands around her face and kissed her. They spent the rest of the night drinking and laughing and talking about the future. Manny already knew all of Mikal's dreams. There was a time one summer night many years ago that they talked about the very same things. Back then, neither of them really thought of girls.

"You see," Mikal explained. "The point of making music isn't to make money or to become famous. The only reason to sing a song or play a melody is to move a person's soul. If anything I create can mean something, anything, to anyone else and they find some sort of comfort or inspiration then I've accomplished what every artist should strive to accomplish."

"We create art to connect souls. That's what I was born to do. Money is a tool to buy time, that's all. With time, I can invest my energy. Fame is also a tool so that my work can be spread and hopefully reach the people that need to hear it."

Manny believed that Mikal truly believed in what he said. There weren't a lot of people left that had the kind of faith that Mikal had. Someone too innocent for this world, Manny thought. He watched the pair giggle about something and take mouthfuls of liquor between breaths.

By the time the group stumbled out of the bar, Mikal and his girlfriend were happier than children on Christmas. Living in a big city has its perks. The two guys lived in the same building just a block away. The girl lived across town but agreed to walk them to their apartment before calling a cab. Mikal stumbled up the stairs gathering his keys then disappeared behind a glass door. Manny sat on the steps, pulling out a cigarette.

"Can I get one of those?" the girl asked him. He extended his hand out. She gripped it in her lips and leaned closer to him. He lit it for her, illuminating her face. She wasn't nearly as drunk as she was leading Mikal to believe. The light from the flames danced on the skin exposed from her top.

She backed away and stood on the edge of the street waiting for her ride. Manny could see the outlines of her chest and hips. Even in the shadows, she was beautiful. He could feel his heart beating.

"You okay?" she asked. Her tone gave her away. Manny had been suspicious that she didn't trust him and with the way she showed her fake concern it was confirmed.

"You don't like me do you?" he asked, avoiding her question.

"Of course I do!" she said, trying to sound sincere. "You're Mikal's best friend."

"Yeah," he said, chuckling. "That's the only reason we ever hang out. If you passed me on the street or saw me in one of your college classes you would avoid me. I can tell. It's not that you don't like me. You don't trust me. Do I scare you?" The pain in his leg began to flare.

"This conversation is scaring me," she said defensively. "It's not like that at all." Her voice trembled when she talked. Manny knew she was just saying the kind phrases in an attempt to avoid confrontation. She was doing her best to be safe. Getting impatient waiting for the taxi, she pulled her phone from her pocket.

Manny stood up from the steps and examined his surroundings. The street was lined with cars collecting morning dew. They looked like silent judges with their unblinking eyes as headlights. *Tonight's audience.* Above him he could see towering walls lined with dark windows and a sliver of a smog filled sky. The street lights lit the area, well, the ones that were not flickering or dead. The streetlights at the intersections blinked periodically and cast a red light through the street. It made the stagnant fog shimmer red. Most importantly, the road was quiet and there were no living eyes watching them.

The girl's face glowed with the faint blue tint of a phone's screen. She was facing the street but he could see her jaw tense. If anything she looked tired but not inebriated. Of course, it'd be easier if she was drunk, after all, she was supposed to be. That's why the plan was for tonight. It didn't really matter though, Manny decided. Mikal was asleep upstairs and wouldn't wake up for hours.

It took two steps to close the distance between them. The girl didn't even react.

Manny's arm went around her neck. As he tightened his grip, he pulled her down to the ground below the tops of all the vehicles, just in case. She threw her arms back at his body and head but each swing missed. He could smell her hair and the top of her head. The sweet scent from her shampoo mixed with the industrial fumes from rusted cars and untended gutters. She made no sound as the world turned black for her.

Manny pushed the unconscious girl off his lap, spitting out strands of hair that got caught in his teeth. That wasn't hard, he thought to himself. He took a deep breath, enjoying the air of their cold humid morning. The world slept while he lifted the girl and headed down the street toward his car.

The small vehicle used to be his parents'. Dents and paintless patches littered the exterior of the light green metal frame. It took an effort to open the door with the girl in his arms but he managed. Resting on the floor was the tape that he had prepared earlier. He set the girl down on the worn and ripped back seat. Then he took the tape and secured her legs and hands.

"We'll get you home soon," he whispered to her, taking a step back to inspect his work. Even in his decaying car, she was beautiful. He made his way into the driver's seat and turned the car on. He took one final look to make sure no one had seen him. Satisfied, he turned the car on and drove away.

Manny took note of the time as they left the city. It was four in the morning. The quiet towers and silent corridors of empty streets passed by in a blur. It took another half hour to reach the woods that lined the property of his parents' house. As a child, these trees used to scare him. In his memories, they were always large and barren. The end of their branches looked like long skinny hands that could scoop a child up by impaling their ends into their chest. *No one would look for his skeleton at the tops of trees.* That's what his mom used to say. He would lay awake at night and think of lost children hanging from the canopy. From the ground, no one would be able to tell a limb apart. Branch or bone? In the light of red moons, a blazing sun, or an overcast sky, the interconnected twisted branches all looked the same.

He turned onto the dirt road and followed its winding path. Even as an adult the trees made him feel cautious. The headlights illuminated the closest edge of the forest but they cast shadows that danced across branches and bushes. Manny always felt there was an evil that lived in those shadows. Watching.

The house emerged from the trees like a curtain blowing in the wind. It was a rather large house for its location. It was two stories tall with a sizable attic. Over the years of Manny's neglect of maintenance, there were roof tiles that needed replacing and the whole building could use a fresh coat of paint. Considering how infrequently he visited, the place was livable.

He pulled his car to the side and onto a graveled area. The backyard lit up revealing a small yard and a playset that was losing the fight against the weather. Just past the yard were more trees and nestled just a few feet flowed a stream that connected to the Hudson somewhere along its path. Manny turned the car off and opened the door.

Immediately, the songs of birds and insects fell onto his ears. This was a comforting noise, a deafening silence, a blanket of familiarity and belonging. He stepped to the back door and opened it to retrieve his new pet. She was laying exactly the same as when he had finished restraining her. He dragged her to the edge of the seat and lifted her over his shoulder. He could smell her sweat from the late night of partying.

At the front of the house, Manny ascended the two steps that lay before the large oak door. He entered the empty house and found the light switch. A light flickered on above his head as the door shut behind him, silencing the wildlife outside.

The house was dust covered with furniture that hadn't been used in years. He'd always meant to move out of the apartment and come back here. Both his parents passed away just last year in a car accident. His father managed to not only take the person Manny loved the most but also the person he hated since he was a kid, all in one drunken mistake.

As Manny made his way to the kitchen. He remembered his mother making big breakfasts, pancakes, eggs, bacon, toast, oatmeal, and sausages. All homemade and all from scratch. Those Sunday mornings were his favorite. His mother always had a smile, even if her makeup didn't cover all the bruises from the night before. His father would smile at least once on those mornings, before his first beer, of course.

He could remember seeing his mother standing over the sink cleaning the dishes. She was always so beautiful, even with the scars. Nothing else in this house felt comforting, but the kitchen. In all the other rooms were memories Manny didn't want to remember. When Manny had told his parents he was joining the military, that was the only time he'd ever gotten any semblance of fatherly love from the man he called dad. An empty house and a lingering smell of his mother's perfume welcomed him home when his deployment ended. It was like his childhood home was waiting for his mom to come home too.

Manny found the door to the basement just past the oversized sink. With his growing number of occupants in the house, it might make more sense to move back home, Manny thought to himself. The door creaked open and the pair descended the stairs.

"Who's that?" a hoarse voice asked from within the dark. Manny set the girl over his shoulder down on the cold floor. The basement wasn't completely finished. The walls and floor were made of rough cement. The ceiling was made of proper materials, drywall, and recessed lighting. Before his passing, his father must've been working on turning the basement into some kind of man cave. Manny found the uncovered light switch near the stairs.

Drywall panels were piled up in one corner behind the stairs along with other various tools. In front of him sat a woman covered in dirt and nothing else. Her skin had turned a faint green and blue over this last year. Manny had been finding it harder and harder to look at her. The girl's hair was matted and had grown down to her chest. The once bright auburn eyes were now husks of brilliant embers that stared back pondering death.

"Who is she?" the woman asked, frustrated this time. "Have you found a replacement?" Manny ignored her and went to work on his new pet.

First, he removed the restraints. She was so still while he pulled the tape from her skin he reached down to her neck and checked for a pulse. Still alive. Next, he removed her clothes. There came some relief when he finally saw her body uncovered like that moment when a roller coaster drops. His heart was racing. The incandescent lights did not do her skin justice.

"Answer me!" the other woman in the room shouted. The chain that was bolted into the ground rattled as she moved. Manny continued to ignore her as he slipped his hands under the new girl and moved her next to his other pet. There was a chain ready already attached to a fresh bolt that he had put into the ground this morning.

He took his time clamping the shackle onto the girl's leg, being careful not to damage her, not yet. As he took a step back he looked down at his two pets. The new one's back was facing him and he noticed a huge blue and green bruise just below her shoulder blades.

"Please just talk to me!" his other pet yelled with tears and anger. Manny knelt down beside his unconscious woman and gently comforted her. She wasn't supposed to be injured during transport.

"Now that you've got another you're going to let me go, right?" his other pet cried. Snot and tears ran down her face. "You said that you would! You said this wouldn't be forever! I don't even have to leave. If I could just go upstairs. I wouldn't leave the house. That's all I'm asking for!"

Manny stood staring down at the begging woman. She was still beautiful, in a sort of broken way, he thought to himself.

"Do you know who this is?" he asked her, replacing the echo of chains rattling with his voice. "This was Mikal's girlfriend. I told you, didn't I? Everyone would forget about you and move on. You've been replaced. Not here, but out there in that world that breeds liars and hypocrites and all sorts of monsters."

Manny watched her face as different emotions filled her heart. She was hurt, clearly, and then sad and finally angry.

"This whore!" she yelled as she tried to hit her with fists of skin and bone. Manny caught her arm before it made contact. "She doesn't deserve Mikal! He was *mine*! Let me kill her. No, let me help paint her body like you paint mine."

"You want to help me?" Manny asked.

"Set me free and we can find all the pretty girls you want," she said, smiling. "Unchain me and I can lure in girls for you. We can work together. I won't rat you out. I won't go to the police. In exchange, I want to help *and* I want to be with Mikal again. The work you do here is art. You've painted me and taken care of me. Honestly, other girls would be so lucky to find themselves down here. It's unfair I've ever been the only one to experience this. I can help."

Manny watched her face while she talked. He was hoping to find a hint of a lie. She was smiling and looked about the happiest she'd looked since he brought her home. He considered her offer.

"If we do that," he pondered. "I'll really have to move here. More people means more food which means more time. I would need you to help me with that... it could work. I never really thought about expanding. You know that if you are lying or trying to betray me I will kill not only you but Mikal too."

"Of course," she responded, maybe a little too quickly. "I know what I'm doing. I'm not as weak or stupid as I look. I don't care about these pretty little sluts. I'll do anything to be with Mikal again. I want to be free."

This all seemed too good to be true, Manny thought to himself. But what's the worst that could happen? He loses his first pet and he'll have to truly replace her? It could be fun. There would need to be a transition period. He had begun to love the chains. The silver extensions of his power across the bare pale skin of bleeding vessels, brought him just as much joy as the paint. With his girl new discoveries were made nearly every night. Not all of them continued, but the ones that did allowed him to sleep better. Manny tried to imagine this girl standing in the halls above covered in nothing but chains and her own blood. His hand was shaking, his mouth was nearly watering, and he thought how hard it would be to let the sight before him become the other. Could he give up either? He wouldn't have too if he had more women.

"You've got a deal, Holly."

[4: 54 A.M.]

Deliberation

AUBREY
October 15, 1999
[1: 07 P.M.]

"On the count of three, we all pull!" Aubrey shouted back to the group. Her hands were wrapped around an electrical extension cable that Manny had found in a janitor's closet. The cable was wrapped around the door handle so tight, she feared it would rip. They were trying to pull open a door to a classroom that still had kids inside. For some reason, their room didn't fill with water and the door hadn't opened.

"We'll push when you do," a faint voice called back to her. The door was sealed shut. She had asked if anyone in the hall had seen someone opening the doors as they completed their test. Everyone said they opened on their own.

"One, two, three!" Aubrey yelled. The group of kids pulled as hard as they could while the other side pushed and kicked and rammed their bodies against the wood. It didn't take Aubrey that long to realize this whole operation was rushed.

After their release from the room, Aubrey inspected all the doors and could hear behind a few the low hum of electricity. Those rooms must have been missed, Aubrey figured. The ones whose rooms hadn't gone up in sparks must've had covers over the outlets. Then there were two classes whose rooms didn't fill with water at all.

To her, however, the biggest hint that this wasn't a perfect execution was that they seemed to have passed the test and yet, one student in their room died. That wasn't a part of the rules. No one in her room should have died. This game they were playing was not fair. She feared it wasn't over.

The frame of the door finally gave in with a loud crack as splinters flew to the ground. Now gathered in the hall, the teenagers cheered their small victory. Aubrey stepped past the excited kids and entered the room. She went to the outlets and confirmed her suspicion. There were plastic covers with the same adhesive that she found on the windows. In the middle of the room sat a pile of broken chairs and desks.

Nearly half the doors had not opened, Aubrey noticed as she went back into the hall. Although her test was not cruel, some of the others seemed impossible. *Cover the blackboard in blood...* Stephen had said. *Create a fire... Present one dead body to the door... Unanimously decide one person to live, the others will die...* Those were just a few tests Stephen had delivered to them over the intercom. What did any of it prove?

"Hey!" Manny yelled, taking her mind away from her questions. "Don't go far!" A pair of kids were making their way out of sight down one of the halls.

"We just want to see if all the doors and windows are sealed," one of them shouted back.

"Don't separate!" Manny commanded. His voice gave Aubrey goosebumps. "Look, we passed that test. Stephen knows we're out in this hall. He knows what we're doing, what we're thinking. For all we know we've left one death trap and entered a new one."

"Do you really think there is more to this?" Evrona asked from the crowd.

"This was planned," Aubrey answered before Manny got the chance. "The windows are sealed. There are rubber strips along the doors. The outlets have covers on them. Then there's the water. This took effort.

Manny's right, we don't know enough to be wandering off or making rash decisions. For all we know, Stephen wasn't working alone."

"We know he wasn't working alone!" the girl whose friend died yelled the words at Aubrey. "Mercy died in that room. If you've forgotten, our task was to find the imposter working with Stephen. We failed, and only when one of us died did the door open."

"That's not what that meant," Aubrey explained. "We passed that test! That's why the door opened at all. We all would have died if I was wrong. What I'm saying is, Stephen's test wasn't some divine order executed by this perfect mastermind of a villain. He made mistakes. These empty rooms without water are proof. These mistakes can either get us killed or we can use them to our advantage."

"How?" Manny asked.

"I'm not sure," she replied, trying to think of a better answer. The teenagers had formed a circle around her and at the slightest hint of uncertainty in her voice exploded into arguments. Aubrey looked to Manny who seemed agitated.

"Let's move everyone to the cafeteria and decide how we want to approach this situation," Manny shouted, silencing everyone. That seemed to be good enough for everyone as they walked down the hall toward the lunch room.

Aubrey found Michelle in the crowd and took a step toward her but something tugged at her arm. It was Evrona.

"We need to talk," Evrona said to Aubrey in a whisper. Michelle approached the two girls. "Without that girl." Evrona snapped.

"Go on without me," Aubrey said to Michelle. The mute girl hesitated but then joined the rest of the kids as they walked away. This was strange to Aubrey. She figured Evrona didn't like her. She didn't really like the short girl very much but the fact she wanted to talk in private was curious. "What do you want?"

"It's about Manny," she said, still whispering even though they were alone in the hall now. "I was in the same room as him when the test began. It's disgusting, the way he takes control and tries to make decisions even after what I saw him do." She paused looking around to make sure they were in fact alone. "All I'm trying to say is this, don't let him take control. It has to be you, or me, or literally anyone else."

"What happened?" Aubrey asked. Her hands were trembling. Evrona shook her head as if to say she couldn't bear remembering. "Well, if you can't tell me what he did, at least tell me what test you guys had."

Aubrey watched Evrona's eyes fill with tears as she turned and walked down the hall. What could have been so bad? Aubrey wondered, if it was bad enough to bother someone like that, it must have been horrible.

Feeling uneasy, Aubrey found her way back to the lunchroom. The main group of students were standing near the back away from the doors she entered from. There was a lot of talking amongst them but in hushed voices. She spotted the group from her room. Maybe going through a traumatic experience formed a bond between them. Maybe they were already friends. Aubrey spotted Michelle standing by herself.

As Aubrey made her way to join her, she felt eyes on her. Sure, the other kids probably felt closer because of all of this, but right now Aubrey felt more like an outsider than she did when the school day started. She could hear their whispers. Some people were saying that she and Michelle were in the room with the imposter. Others said they've only seen her for the first time today. The worst she heard was someone outright saying she murdered that girl. Her face felt warm and she felt she could throw up from all the attention.

These people were not her friends but she'd always had a desire to help. This came out most with Michelle, but she felt it for the others too. Maybe Stephen had a point. If these people couldn't see that she'd *helped* them, then what was the point? No, she thought to herself, that's not why a good person does the right thing.

She knew a person did the right thing just because it was right. She couldn't let herself begin to think like him. Her mind felt foggy. It was the stress, she told herself. Michelle reached out to Aubrey. She couldn't feel the warmth of her fingers as they wrapped around her arm like they had done many times this day. It reminded her of her mom. Standing here beside this girl, Aubrey had never felt so alone. She remembered standing with her mom watching her father throw clothes from a dresser.

Her mom was yelling words filled with anger meant to hurt, whether or not they were true, Aubrey did not know. It didn't matter now, she couldn't remember the words. She could only remember how she felt. The look in her father's eyes as he accepted the pain. Sympathy had grown inside her for him, but whenever she tried to go to him, her mother would grab her arm. Her long thin fingers twisted around her arm like vines adorned with thorns. If she knew the truth of their divorce then maybe she would hate both of them now.

The truth of it was there are no good people and there are no evil people. Aubrey knew that people are a collection of experiences, interpretations of moments, and a malleable heart filled with emotions forged from reactions. She held this belief above most others and tried to be an understanding and reasonable person. Maybe, she wondered, this is why Stephen tested them. If what he said was true, he must have been hurt by someone he trusted. Despite our flaws, people were worth saving. Surely, he knew this, right?

"We have to assume we are still being tested." Drake was standing on a chair using a commanding voice. The kids around her were not paying attention to him. Even his pleas for focus went unheard. When she tried to listen to the crowd, it was a blur of fear, confusion, and anger. One kid next to her was saying over and over that this wasn't really happening. There were voices behind her claiming to have seen Stephen earlier during the day.

"If we all could just calm down." Again, Drake's voice reverberated off the cries and whispers of a stone room full of kids. This wasn't going to work, Aubrey realized. No one was going to listen to him. In all the panic she had lost sight of Evrona and Manny. She scanned the room and found Evrona on one side of the lunchroom and Manny stood alone against the wall near Drake.

"Please!" Drake pleaded with the crowd but with each passing minute the voices grew louder and the anxiety fostered itself. For Aubrey the only person that could take control of this situation was Manny. His voice was commanding enough that people listened, but looking at him now, he'd changed.

What Evrona said still bothered Aubrey. Of all the tests they went through if they passed they must have done nothing. That was the real test Aubrey realized, to do nothing. Is life worth living if we have to sacrifice our friends? This is the question Stephen must have been asking. The answer was obviously no. Then what did Manny do in their room that scared Evrona?

Aubrey pulled her arm away from Michelle. She could ask Manny for help, but she would try herself first. Drake clearly was not a leader, no matter how nice he looked or how much he wanted to be one. Aubrey walked through the crowd of kids and reached the poor boy pleading with everyone. She turned her back to the white stone wall and looked out at the scene.

The kids had formed a semi-circle around Drake as if they wanted to listen to him but refused. With them, all bunched together there seemed to be so many. Aubrey knew this was less than half the kids she had seen throughout the day. So many lives, she thought to herself. *No wonder they're scared.*

Behind the crowd, tables and chairs were being pushed against the opposite wall where the doors to the hall led.

To her left was the line where they would have gotten food earlier. She felt sick even though she hadn't eaten. Beyond the line was the kitchen. The lights were off now. Whoever it was serving them was long gone by now. To her right was a great big window reminding them of the stone walls that covered the outside of the building. This was the biggest mystery for her. Out of all the preparation, this one confused her. Unfortunately, she did not have the time to figure it out.

Although Aubrey wanted to use her voice to get their attention, she wasn't sure she could. Something inside her felt like it was missing. She looked over at Michelle and wondered if this was how she felt. Her stomach felt like flames flickering as her throat tightened, but only when she thought about talking. The image of the girl drowning flashed before her eyes.

It hurt Aubrey, more than she would ever know, but if someone didn't take control of this situation things would only get worse. She couldn't let that happen.

"I know you're all scared." Aubrey's voice resonated against glass and rock back to her. She didn't even recognize it. "I don't know if any of you have even realized but less than half of all the classrooms passed their tests." Evrona and Manny gave Aubrey their attention.

"We don't know what this means," Aubrey continued. "For all we know Stephen has received his answers. He could be miles from here leaving us to carry his acts of torture to our graves. I don't plan on dying here!" This sentiment got the attention of a few other kids who quieted themselves. "When I woke up this morning I didn't know that evil existed. I assumed most people were a mix of good and bad, but this, this is something different. This takes someone truly evil. We have to assume Stephen was working alone or with a small number of people. There are over a hundred of us here. If he can trap us in here, then we can get out."

More kids were paying attention to Aubrey and for a moment she felt a bit of hope. "If we all work together we can find a way out. As I said, there were flaws in his tests. There have to be flaws in his trap. The one unknown we have is whether or not we're alone in here. I know Kim has voiced her opinion that Stephen wasn't working alone and that one of us is working for him. I say this isn't true. More to the point, even if it were true it doesn't matter. We still outnumber them. They are only human and I haven't seen any weapons."

All of the kids in the lunchroom were now quiet and listening to Aubrey. "This is just like the test, we've got two options. We can stay here in this lunchroom for as long as we can, hoping that our parents or anyone else notice we're missing. We don't know how long that will take. Our other option is we take turns forming teams to scout for holes in whatever has surrounded the school. That way, if Stephen is still here, he won't get all of us in another trap, and maybe we can outsmart him."

The last sentence left a smile on Aubrey's face. The teenagers seemed to agree with her as they nodded their heads and began to talk amongst themselves again. The lunchroom began to fill with voices of confidence instead of fear. This was the last time Aubrey would feel this sense of happiness.

"You're wrong!" Manny's commanding voice scared Aubrey and silenced the room. Aubrey felt ill as her eyes met his. There was anger behind his words, she feared it had existed this whole time, and he was staring directly at her.

[1: 32 P.M.]

Culling of Flames

MANNY
October 15, 1999
[1: 32 P.M.]

Aubrey's hands were shaking, Manny noticed, as he walked toward her. He couldn't stand by and listen to her any longer. There was a part of him that wanted to believe what she was saying.

"We've lost innocent people already," he explained to her. He could feel the eyes of everyone in the room on him. "This is a game, and we are losing, and will continue to lose if we don't end it. If we do what you want, we'll be playing into more traps. Stephen is here with us. Can't you feel it?"

In truth, ever since Manny had encountered Stephen in this lunchroom he'd felt another presence in his thoughts. It was as if Stephen had invited himself into his head and was making himself at home. Even now, Manny's vision felt foggy and his movements seemed to be happening in slow motion.

"Stephen is an infection," Manny continued, turning to face the crowd. A few kids were nodding in agreement with what he was saying. He wondered if they were feeling the same sensations as him. "The only solution is to play the game on his rules and hope to win. We all know it. We're being tested right now. Aubrey, you may have been right once, but that was just luck. I'm not claiming to know exactly what's going on here but we can't make guesses. I'm not dying because you want to take unnecessary risks. We have to find Stephen and kill him."

Manny watched as half of the students cheered. The other half looked scared and uncertain. Aubrey was right about one thing, they outnumbered Stephen. If they could find him they could kill him and end this. After all, he's only human, right? He looked back to Aubrey wondering how she'd feel about his proposition.

For the first time, he actually took her appearance in. She was tall for a girl. Her face seemed small in her long dark brown hair. The combination of her dark hair and light skin made her reddish brown eyes shimmer. To him, her clothes looked a little old fashioned. She was wearing a shirt with the neck hole much larger than it needed to be with her size. It exposed one shoulder at a time and he could see a red tank top underneath. Manny imagined the thin red straps were blood trails running down her shoulders.

He had to take a deep breath. Ever since his test he kept seeing images of the female form bathing in deep red pools. For a moment, this same scene appeared in his mind with Aubrey, but it made him feel guilty. With a sick feeling in his stomach, he turned his attention back to the crowd.

"We can safely assume Stephen is not here in the lunchroom," Manny shouted over the rumble of voices. "I'm going out into the school to find where he is hiding. I am going to find Stephen. We will never be safe until he is gone or dead. If we don't find him at least we know what we can't do. If we do find him, well, I'm sure we all know what we must do. Who's with me?"

As the room erupted in eager volunteers, Manny felt elated. This feeling of being in control was familiar to him. "I'll take a group of four with me to go find Stephen."

"I'll go," one kid shouted over everyone else. Manny recognized him from the same room Aubrey was tested in. Two guys behind the boy agreed they would go too.

"What's your name?" Manny asked, approaching them. The rest of the room began to talk amongst themselves. The three kids in front of him looked strong. The one who spoke first was tall with strong arms and a square face to match. He told Manny his name was Ben and his friends were Chris and Josh.

"We'll end this," Josh said to Manny as if he needed to say the words to believe it. He was shorter than Ben but had a bigger frame. The other kid, Chris, was just as tall as Manny but didn't look to have a single muscle on him. Manny was sure he hung out with these guys for protection. Using bullies to do the dirty work was fine with him.

"Yeah," Manny responded, hiding his annoyance. "This is going to be dangerous. We're not going out back and stealing some nerd's lunch money like some punks. This is a man who is okay with killing children. He won't hesitate to stop us and we have to be prepared for whatever is waiting for us. Yes, we're playing a game, but we've seen how important this all is to him. It needs to be just as real and important to us."

The group of boys nodded in agreement. Manny could see the fear in their eyes. For the first time today, he felt older than the rest of them. *These are just kids,* he thought to himself. He looked to his own hands. They seemed rougher and bigger than the guys around him.

"I'm coming too," the voice of a girl said behind Manny. He turned half expecting it to be Aubrey but it was another student from the same test she had been in.

"I'm Kim," the girl said. She was nearly a whole foot shorter than him. Her short black hair exposed her ears which were riddled with glistening jewelry. She had a small face with a strong expression. He liked her prominent freckles that peaked out through her smudged black makeup. She was clearly not strong enough to beat anyone up, but the expression on her face convinced Manny she wouldn't stand down from a fight.

"We can use as many eyes as we can get," Manny said to her, placing his hand on her shoulder. "When we leave this room, we're a team, but I'm in charge. If anything seems to go wrong, do whatever I say, okay?" He directed the question to their small group. They all nodded. Satisfied Manny made his way over to Aubrey.

She was standing near Michelle talking to her about going through the back of the lunchroom and gathering all the food. He may not trust her to solve this Stephen problem, but he could find a use for her.

"Hey," he said to get her attention. He watched her body tense at the sound of his voice. Was she really that afraid of him? "Look, I know we don't exactly agree with each other but I'm ending this. Keep everyone here preoccupied with whatever you think is important. I don't want anyone in the halls. If we see anyone I want to be confident they are either Stephen or someone he's working with. After all, none of us knows what he looks like. I have a feeling we'll know when we see him."

He half expected her to fight back, but she just nodded without acknowledging him. *Good*, he thought to himself, *she's learning*. He felt odd with the last thought but ultimately agreed with his own sentiment. They should all be thanking him for what he was about to do. Instead, they were doing what Aubrey was saying.

Frustrated, he turned and headed for the cafeteria storage area. His group followed closely behind. He made his way to the counters where the kids would grab their food. Manny vaulted the counter and landed in the dark. The rest of the group stood by the counter.

"Wait there," Manny shouted back at them. He could hear a faint hum coming from a refrigerator. In the shadows, he could make out large coolers and long metal tables. The room was large with red tiles on the floor. What he needed was in the back, he assumed. It was unsettling quiet back here in the dark and for some reason, he felt he was being watched.

As he made his way to the back, he kept an eye on the corners of the large kitchen equipment. Anyone could be just around a corner waiting for him. Subconsciously, he was crouching and stepping as if each step would wake a monster only he could see. The further he went into the kitchen, the darker it got, making it seem that the shadows were moving around, but there was no noise except for his own heartbeat.

Finally, he reached where he thought he could find what he was looking for. He placed his hand on one of the drawers and opened it.

Even though he was trying to be quiet the sound of metal objects hitting each other resonated throughout the room. He looked around making sure he was still alone. He didn't see any living being but spotted a door with the words EMERGENCY EXIT printed in red. He paused wondering if the door may be an exit for them. Either way, they would still need what was in the drawer. He put his hand in, feeling for any handles.

In total there were six knives. Four of them were standard chef's knives while the other two were serrated bread knives. Manny gathered them up and moved over to the door. If he pushed on the door and it opened, he could be the savior of the day, maybe he could go out and find some help, or maybe he could just leave and forget about all of this.

If there was one thing Manny was certain of, it was that all of what had happened to him today was not his problem. Sure, he was there for the whole ordeal, but this Stephen kid had said he used to be a student here. To Manny, this all seemed like some sort of revenge. For what, he wasn't exactly sure, but who wouldn't want to torture their old bullies? That piece of paper with his schedule on it made it seem like Manny was supposed to be here but this whole time something felt off. Forging something like that would be easy. He didn't belong here. This was all he kept thinking.

Why should I help them?

Manny put his fist on the push handle and applied pressure. The latch clicked and the door moved outward. A small gust of cold air reached in giving him goosebumps. Through the small sliver between the door and its frame, Manny could only see darkness. He stepped into the door pushing it just a little further. Some light spilled over his shoulders and he could see more clearly.

Outside there was just a wall of solid cement, he expected that, but there seemed to be a little space between the walls of the school and their stone prison. This could be how Stephen is moving through the school without being seen, Manny thought to himself. This was the closest he'd been to the cement. Something compelled him to reach out and touch it.

With the point of the knives in his right hand, he extended his arm. As he moved closer the door swung open and hit the side of the building with a thud. He was standing with one foot in the building and the other on concrete. Deep down he feared leaving, he realized. At least here he had a purpose. At least here people listened to him. If he left this building he might find that he was someone terrible. His hand was shaking as the tip of one of the blades made contact with the outer wall. He stopped.

At first, he was convinced his mind was tricking him. The tip of the blade seemed to penetrate the wall as if it wasn't really there. He pushed his hand further. A shimmer of gold light seemed to engulf the blade as it moved forward. Yellow flakes that looked like embers from a forgotten fire fell onto his face. They were warm like a morning shower. As they made contact, they seemed to crumble into nothing.

The wall wasn't real.

They weren't really trapped inside the building. He pulled his knife back inside. He had a decision to make. Of course, there was a part of him that wanted to free the school right then and there, but something bothered him about that. Stephen would get away with what he'd done to him.

If they left now, Manny was sure Stephen would avoid any consequences. Would Manny be able to accept that? No, that couldn't happen. Manny stepped back inside the kitchen and made sure to close the door slowly so it made no noise. He made his way to the front of the kitchen forgetting to be afraid of the shadows. Once he reached the counter he spilled his spoils out for the group to see. At first, no one spoke, but then Manny asked, "remember what I said? This isn't something that can be resolved with words."

One after the other they all reached down and grabbed at a handle. With two knives left Manny put one into his pocket and the other he held for everyone to see. He jumped over the counter being careful with the blades and walked to the doors that led to the halls. There were a group of students piling chairs and tables against the door. "We're going out there!" Manny shouted to no one in particular.

One of the kids began to object but spotted the knife in his hand. Manny pointed it up at his face and told him to move. Another kid that just set a chair in front of the door walked up to Manny. "Calm down dude!" he yelled. "We just put this stuff here. No one should be going out there anyways."

"I refuse to stay here like rats trapped in a pet store," Manny yelled at the kid. "I thought just a little bit ago everyone was so on board with finding Stephen. What happened? Get scared?" The sound of shoes against linoleum filled the room as students began to gather around them.

"Manny," Aubrey said behind him, her voice full of fear. "What are you doing?"

"I'm trying to save everyone!" he shouted back at her. One of the bigger kids took a step toward Manny as he spoke. Ben came up beside him and pointed his own knife at the boy. The rest of the group followed suit and pulled their knives up as a defense.

"We're not your enemy," Aubrey said to him, this time her words held sadness. He could tell she only talked to comfort herself. All of his anger and frustration went into his arm as he slashed at the young man standing in his way. The boy threw his arms up to defend himself and Manny closed his eyes as his arm swung down. He could feel the handle vibrate as it sliced through his shirt and made contact with his skin.

The kid screamed and stumbled back into the pile of chairs and tables. Manny opened his eyes and turned his back to the sight. The other kid that tried stopping Manny ran over to help the injured boy. Manny flung his knife out toward Aubrey. Blood flicked off the blade and landed on some of the students. A drop managed to reach her cheek. He watched for a moment as it ran down her face and fell to the floor. His heart was racing.

"We are leaving," Manny said to her. These were not the words he wanted to say. In his heart, he wanted to stay, he wanted to feel the warmth of her skin as his fingers rubbed the blood across her face. He had to stop himself. He took a deep breath trying to stop his heart from exploding and his mind from going too far. "And by the way, there's no food in the kitchen. None of you will survive for very long if you follow her."

[1: 57 P.M.]

Forlorn Hands

AUBREY
October 15, 1999
[2: 42 P.M.]

Aubrey looked over at the coolers shrouded in shadows. Her fingers stuck to each other as she attempted to wipe the blood off on her jeans. She sat upright and looked at her work. The kid's arm was wrapped in her shirt which was now pink and red all over. Someone had lent her their belt to be tied around his arm too. He'd lost a lot of blood and even now there was a steady stream leaking from his bandage. This was the second person she'd patched up today. She hoped it would be the last.

Manny and the others had been gone about an hour now. For all she knew, they weren't even in the building and instead, managed to find a way out. She had to believe that Manny wasn't heartless enough to leave them behind. She had to.

She reached up and pressed her arm against her forehead, brushing her hair aside. No one seemed to want to be involved in helping the boy. Most of the kids weren't even standing around them anymore. It was like, if they just ignored it, they wouldn't be a part of it. *We're all being tested*, Aubrey thought to herself. They all needed to start acting like it.

She wasn't sure if she believed they were only being tested by Stephen, but they were being tested as people for certain. Their actions now would define what kind of people they would grow to become. More immediately, it would determine if they survived. With that thought, she looked back down at the boy on the floor. His face was pale and his breathing was slow. She wasn't sure if he was even conscious at this point.

Without the proper tools or help, he wasn't going to make it through the night. She glanced over at the doors to the hall wondering if maybe there was a needle with thread somewhere in the nurse's office. The blockade was back in front of the doors and she wasn't going to hurt anyone in an attempt to leave. The remaining students seemed content to live the rest of their days in this room by the way they were calm and settled.

It was so frustrating.

Aubrey watched the boy's new bandage change to a darker gray. As she stood from kneeling her knees cracked and her calves throbbed. If he was going to last long enough to get real help, she would need those medical supplies from the office. She looked around the room.

Michelle was standing on the other side from her. The mute had helped Aubrey with bandaging the boy. In her oversized clothes and blood on her hands, she looked like a child learning to be a nurse. Her eyes were on the boy on the ground and Aubrey knew without asking that she had come to the same conclusion.

The majority of the kids had gathered in groups and made themselves comfortable. Only one person stood alone, seeming just as annoyed with the rest as she was, Evrona. The short girl hadn't moved after Manny's altercation. Aubrey wondered how much fear a person had to feel to freeze them in time.

Aubrey tapped Michelle on the shoulder and motioned toward the girl in black. Michelle took a look and nodded. Without really knowing if she understood Aubrey walked over to Evrona. This small girl had been nothing but mean to her all day and now she was going to ask her for help.

"Hey, Evrona," Aubrey said, pressing her shoulder against the wall where the girl was looking. Evrona flinched. "We've got a boy over here that Manny hurt. He's not going to last much longer. The cut was deep and he's lost a lot of blood." She lifted her hands showing them stained and beginning to crust. Evrona didn't seem to hear her. She just continued to stare at nothing.

"Look," Aubrey said, trying to comfort her. "I don't know what happened between you and Manny but he's gone now. I need you. That boy over there, he needs you. I don't know why, but people around here seem to listen to you. I mean when you first talked to me you terrified me. I thought you would kill me. You were just so intimidating and fierce." Aubrey tried to smile and lean down so she could see her face. Evrona's black hair was blocking most of it. "I've got one girl who can't talk to me, please don't become another. Besides, I've got a plan and I need your help."

"Oh yeah," Evrona said, breaking her silence. "What's your plan?"

"Basically, all we really have to do is wait long enough for the school buses to arrive. Even if there was food in those coolers, which I don't know if it's smart to believe Manny, we don't even need it. When they realize no one is coming out of the building they will call the police and then they'll call the military and get us out of here. Worst case, it takes a few hours for everyone to get here sometime tonight. Best case we get out of here as soon as the police arrive which could take only a few hours. It's just a waiting game. Someone has to notice all these kids just disappeared. Not even mentioning the teachers. Where are all of them? For all we know, someone has already been notified of any one of us missing."

Aubrey had come to these conclusions while she was helping the injured boy. "Put more simply, Stephen wanted to perform an experiment, but it's impossible to completely isolate us."

"You really are stupid," Evrona responded. "That's not an escape plan. What you want us to do is cower in this room while Manny and

Stephen both trample over us. We'll all be dead before anyone notices we're missing."

"Why are you like this?" Aubrey asked, showing her frustration. "What's wrong with you? We have people here that are counting on us. I've said it before and I'll say it again, this whole setup, although clever, was executed by an imperfect human man. He's not a god." Evrona looked up into Aubrey's eyes.

"What makes you so sure?" Evrona asked her. Aubrey felt a pit form at the bottom of her stomach. If she told this girl that she'd seen Stephen at the beginning of the school day others might think it was suspicious. Before she could defend herself Evrona continued. "You weren't there. You didn't have to see what he did. Sure, I asked him to help, but I didn't know what he'd do."

"Please," Aubrey begged as she went to touch one of the girl's folded arms but missed. "Tell me then, what happened in your test. Help me understand because right now he's out there doing whatever he wants. For some reason, a lot of these kids listen to him. They're scared. If maybe you and I work together we can get them all on our side. Tell me what happened."

Aubrey watched Evrona's face twist with emotion as she tried to suppress her anger. Eventually, all that surfaced was tears and Aubrey felt she would never be able to truly understand her. The once mean girl stood before her, raining tears onto the floor, vulnerable and weak. "Okay," Aubrey said. "It doesn't matter. What matters now is that you are here and we can stop him before he hurts anyone else. Michelle and I are going to go to the nurse's office and get some supplies. All I need you to do is hold down the fort here. Just make sure no one does anything reckless. Can you do that?"

Aubrey grabbed the girl's shoulder and squeezed. It took a few sniffles, but Evrona managed a nod. That was all she could expect from her, Aubrey thought as she walked back to Michelle. As much as she wanted to stay and take care of everyone, there was one boy who needed more help than anyone. There just wasn't enough time for everyone.

As Aubrey approached Michelle she looked down at the bandage. It was completely soaked through and a new pool of blood was forming beneath him. Michelle caught her eye and shook her head. *They really were running out of time.*

"You and I are going to the nurse's office," Aubrey said to her, unwilling to acknowledge the possibility that it may be too late for the kid. Michelle nodded and they both began to make their way to the doors. She feared repeating the same scene from earlier but no one seemed to care this time.

Aubrey moved to one end of the table and motioned for Michelle to help her. The two girls lifted the long cafeteria table shifting all the chairs on top. With one step to her left, the chair fell to the ground with loud clangs of metal against linoleum. Whether or not anyone took notice of their exit, Aubrey would never know. She dropped the table and hurried through to the door. She and Michelle squeezed through, entering the halls.

They were greeted by an unfamiliar silence. In the lunchroom, all the voices and movements against the floor seemed to be magnified, but out here there was nothing. The hall somehow felt different like a thin red mist had spread taking over the air. Aubrey closed her eyes, shook her head, and when she opened them again, it was gone.

"Weird," she said without thinking. Michelle gave her a look that told her she knew why she'd said what she had. The two girls began to make their way down the hall. The sound of their shoes echoed off the metal walls of lockers and around corners of still air. With each step, the mist moved around their feet causing a sort of wave that silently crashed against the bottoms of locker doors.

"I've been feeling different all day long," Aubrey said to Michelle. "I know we've been through a lot. It's strange to think that only a few hours ago we just met. I still know nothing about you. Last night I lay in bed wondering if I was going to hate my classes or maybe meet some new friends. I miss my old friends. There was Seth, he was funny. I know we're, like, still in high school but he cared about me, ya know?

"The last time I saw him was in front of my old house. He had come over the night before we were supposed to leave. It feels like years ago, but that was only two nights back. He had said we'd still be friends and that if I ever needed him, he'd be there. He smiled at me and made me believe him. I don't think he meant to lie. I need him now. I feel so alone. I'm sorry, Michelle. I didn't mean it like that. It's just, you seem like you're in your own world. The way you ignore everything. We watched someone drown and neither of us cried. That hurts the most. I'm ready to feel the pain, but who will help everyone if I let myself become useless?

"I've always been like this, unwilling to let something hurt me if it means someone else might suffer more. I've seen my dad hit my mom so hard her whole arm turned purple. I've seen my mom try to kill my dad with a knife. That's why we moved. That's why she cries every night. I still haven't cried. I just wanted them to be okay. I'll be fine. What matters more is that maybe there's something I can do to help. Crying won't solve anything. Being hurt by something that didn't even happen to me? Where's the use in it? Why waste time feeling sorry for myself? I can be useful. I can help."

The two girls rounded the corner and Michelle grabbed Aubrey's arm. They stopped and faced each other. The girl who couldn't speak attempted to say something. Only groans and strain escape, like having the worst sore throat ever. Aubrey shook her head. It was enough. For a moment she didn't feel alone. It made her sad that it didn't make her feel any better. If she told Michelle this, it would just hurt both of them. So, she smiled back.

"You can feel it though, can't you?" Aubrey asked her. "Like, there's someone else in our heads, tempting us. This should probably make me feel less alone. I feel more isolated now than I ever have. We'll figure this all out though. Maybe we'll cry after it's all done. We've got people to help."

Michelle pulled the feather from earlier out of her pocket. She motioned it in front of Aubrey trying to say something. Then moved it to her chest. With her other hand, she pointed to Aubrey then to the feather, and then to herself. Whatever she was trying to say Aubrey couldn't understand. She shook her head.

Aubrey turned away from the mute. She appreciated her attempt at making her feel better. The truth of it, what she hid because to her it was pointless, was that she was terrified. After all, who was she? Just some girl with her own problems and no real strengths.

"Thanks," Aubrey said back to Michelle as she walked away. "That boy is waiting on us."

The two girls approached the door to enter the office. As Aubrey's fingers wrapped around the handle, she wondered if Manny would be inside. The thought made her muscles freeze. This whole time she knew she needed to be cautious of him since she found him with Michelle. Everything was different now. He had terrified Evrona and could be the reason a student ends up dead. Regardless of how he was involved with Michelle, he was dangerous. With Manny in mind, she slowly turned the handle and listened inside. After a few moments, the only sounds she could hear were the muffled screams of all the kids who'd drowned.

Her heart felt like it fell inside her chest. She squeezed her fist and shook the sounds from her head. The silence allowed her mind to wander. There wasn't any time to be afraid, she thought to herself.

Gathering her courage, Aubrey entered the room and made her way to the back. She let her mind focus on her goal, ignoring everything else in the room. It was dark with a tint of green cast onto everything from the little light that bounced from the carpet. Without hesitation, she threw the nurse's office door open and made her way to the medicine cabinet. It took her a few moments to gather stitches, bandages, and some medicines to clean the wound.

With all the supplies pressed against her chest, she ran from the room. Michelle was waiting by the door to the offices holding the door open. Aubrey ran through the offices and out into the hall. The two girls jogged until they reached the doors to the lunch room. She hoped no one barricaded the doors.

"Help me," Aubrey said to Michelle as she turned the handle and pressed her shoulder against the large wooden door. Sure enough, someone had put the tables and chairs back. When Michelle slammed her shoulder against the wood they heard them fall to the ground just as they had before. It took both of them, but they managed to get back in. Aubrey had work to do.

She squeezed her body through the wall and the tables being careful with the supplies in her arms. Michelle was right behind her. The two girls out of breath found the boy just on the other side of the tables and got straight to work. The old bandage was a dark red. *We're too late?*

It didn't matter. Aubrey dropped to her knees, let the supplies fall from her arms beside her, and got to work. She unwound the old bandage. The boy flinched in pain. *Good,* Aubrey thought to herself, *he's still alive.* Quickly, she took the antibiotic and spread it through his wound. Satisfied she took the needle and thread and did her best. It wasn't perfect and with each poke, the boy winced and moaned. She didn't like hurting him. After a few minutes of careful work, she tied off the last bit of thread and ripped the remainder with her teeth. Finally, she took the clean bandages and wrapped them around his arm. It felt like a blur. It was done.

Her knees ached as she fell to the side. Michelle had been with her through every hand movement either guiding or helping to make sure Aubrey did a good job. The two girls sat beside the boy feeling like he was going to be okay.

A loud thud echoed into the room as something from outside the lunchroom slammed against the doors. Aubrey felt her heart once again fall into her stomach. Her neck tensed as she looked at Michelle. Aubrey's back was to the door. Whatever it was, Michelle was going to see it first. She watched her eyes while she listened to the sound of the tables screeching against the floors and the remaining chairs clattered around her. Michelle's autumn eyes held a fear Aubrey did not think existed.

"Look, what I've found!" Manny shouted with his commanding voice that gave Aubrey chills. The fear she felt would not allow her to look. Her only reaction was a quiet *no*. Her voice so soft that not even ghosts would be able to hear her.

[3: 51 P.M.]

Dreams of Melodies

MANNY
October 15, 1999
[2: 03 P.M.]

The handle of the knife sat comfortably in Manny's hand as he opened the door to the front offices. The blood falling down Aubrey's face like a red tear kept appearing in his head. It made him feel sick that he couldn't shake the image. At the same time, he knew he didn't want to forget it. Deep down he even wanted to go back and see her again.

"What do we do if we find him?" Kim asked. The group stepped inside the room as quietly as they could. Manny looked at the girl thinking she was cute. She had short hair and not a single light brown strand reached her shoulders. She was tall, skinny, and looked like she never spent time outside. Her face made him angry, but he couldn't place why. It could be the way her eyes were just a little too close together or how her mouth seemed abnormally low on her chin. He kept trying to imagine the same line of red on her face but it just didn't make her look better.

"Like you guys said earlier," Manny responded, hiding his annoyance. "We end this."

"But what does that mean?" the girl asked. He wondered if she was trying to be annoying.

"Does it even matter what it means?" he asked through his teeth. "When we find him we'll know what to do. Are you scared or something?" The boys looked to each other for any sign of weakness and Kim said confidently that she wasn't. "We're out here right now to save everyone. We're the heroes, or at least, we will be when we find Stephen. Everyone split up and search these rooms."

Manny's first find was a panel with four light switches on it. He flipped them all on and the room lit up. At surface level, it looked like an ordinary school office. The dull green carpet and dark woods made it feel cramped. The boys headed down the hall to check the back offices leaving Manny alone with Kim.

"Why did you come?" Manny asked her. "Earlier you seemed really mad at Aubrey, what was up with that?" She explained what had happened in their room and how they passed the test. When she talked about her friend, she strained to hold back tears.

"I can still see her eyes," she explained coming to the end. "She was looking right at me, begging me to help her. I blame that new girl. She made the decision. She made everyone panic. Maybe if we weren't so scared, she could've gotten a better breath. I blame everyone else in that room too. Those idiots in the back were there, fighting amongst themselves. They're bullies. If we had one of the other tests, I don't doubt they would have sacrificed anyone to live. I blame Stephen the most. We wouldn't have been in that situation, to begin with, if it wasn't for him."

"So, when you were asking what we were going to do, you wanted to make sure we were going to make him pay?" Manny asked her, already knowing the answer.

"Yes," she said, moving some papers around on a desk. "I want him dead."

The boys walked back to the front. Manny gave them a questioning look and Ben shook his head. "Is there anywhere you can think of where they might be?" Manny asked the group.

"Not on this side of the building," Josh responded. "This is the main building with all the classrooms. There's the auditorium and gym through that connecting hallway. Plenty of places to hide."

"We'll look there," Manny said, remembering that was where he first entered the school. Kim, being the closest to the door, pulled it open. As the air entered the room, a red mist followed. It seemed heavy only gathering on the ground but it was clearly flowing like a slow moving red stream. No one spoke even though they were all thinking the same thing.

This fog had been present in their minds ever since this morning. It had started as a gray veil over every thought or image in their head. Throughout the day it had turned red. They all assumed this was because of what was happening. No one would be able to think clearly with all the tests and death. Seeing it moving along the floor now terrified every single one of them. It was real and it couldn't be.

Manny moved first. He exited the offices and followed the red river. He heard the office door close behind him along with the patter of footsteps. The only goal he had was to find the source of this mist. It had to lead them to Stephen. As they walked, the red mist stained their shoes and pants with each step through the halls.

They found themselves standing in the windowed hall. On the opposite side of the hall, the doors were propped open. The fog was rushing out meaning they were getting close to the source. The room on the other side was covered in darkness. Through the glass, stone walls stared back at them. Manny wondered where the illusion had come from. If Stephen was capable of pulling off something like this, what else could he do?

He knew Aubrey was convinced Stephen wasn't some kind of god, but if she knew he somehow surrounded the school in imaginary walls, what would she think? Manny took the first step into the hall.

Manny felt the fog in his head thicken and the closer he got to the other end of the hall, his legs felt heavier. He looked back and the others seemed to be feeling the same way. Josh had a hand on the left wall holding himself up. The other two boys were hunched over and breathing deeply. To Manny, it felt like someone had pulled a large blanket over his body and was trying to pull him to the ground.

"You'll pass out if you get any closer," a voice said coming from the darkness. Manny recognized the voice from the intercom.

"Stephen?" he asked, straining to keep his legs from buckling. "What's happening to us?"

From the dark, three people stepped out one by one. Among them stood a tall woman with long blonde hair. She was wearing a blouse and suit pants and looked like a teacher, but like she didn't want to be wearing clothes. They were barely holding onto her body and Manny could see she wasn't wearing anything underneath. She was taller than him by a few inches and her thick hair flowed all the way down to her knees. The way she was staring down at him disturbed Manny. Her face was hauntingly white and thin. She was smiling. Standing beside her was an older looking man much shorter than her. He was thin with short black hair. He was also wearing clothes a teacher would wear, a blue button-up and black slacks. Unlike the girl, his clothes fit him and the look he had on his face. In his eyes, Manny could see he was enjoying the situation. The hair on his head and arms were standing straight up as he had just been struck by lightning. In front of both of them, a younger boy was staring down at the group of kids. This boy was Stephen. He was the same kid he had talked to in the lunchroom. He didn't like the way his silver eyes were watching him. It was like he was trying to decide what to do with them. Pondering their fates as if his suffering was somehow connected.

"That's enough," Stephen said back to one of the adults behind him. The group that was with Manny were all on their hands and knees struggling not to fall to the floor. Manny was the last one with his head angled to see the group before them. He could see the tall girl's legs were shaking. Whatever was happening to the kids was also affecting the three still standing. "Ed," Stephen said in a stern voice turning to look at the man beside him. "We're still not completely immune and I don't want these kids to die here, at least not by your hand."

Manny's head became so heavy he couldn't keep it up. He watched as sweat dripped onto the floor and his arms began to buckle. The knife in his hand hurt just to touch.

"Fine," Ed responded to Stephen. The overbearing feeling suddenly disappeared. It was still hard to breathe but Manny managed to move his body to sit down and catch his breath. The red mist swirled around his body.

"Why do you even have those?" Stephen asked, pointing to the blade in his hand. "Is that for me? Why are you even here? You should still be in the lunchroom getting control of the situation."

"What are you talking about?" Manny managed to ask.

"Yeah, what is he talking about, Manny?" Kim asked, throwing her anger directly at Manny.

"Have any of you even been listening to me?" Stephen asked, frustrated. "I know the future. Right now, Manny should be in that lunchroom gathering support and taking care of everyone. I'll need his support later. This is not that complicated." Stephen looked back at the tall girl with a confused look. She responded with a shrug. "If it wasn't for Edgar here we'd never even noticed you guys approaching. So what, was the plan to come and attack us with a couple of kids and knives? You weren't even going to use the gun that I reminded you of earlier? Too easy? Or is it you don't have the guts to kill me yourself and you wanted these kids behind you to do your dirty work? I thought you were someone that just got stuff done even if it was hard to do. That's why you were chosen after all. I mean that's my best guess anyway, it's the only conclusion that makes sense. Say something."

Any trust the kids behind him had in him was gone. It didn't matter if what Stephen said was true, they wouldn't believe him if he refuted. "Honestly kid," Manny responded, staring directly into Stephen's silver eyes. "I don't know what you're talking about."

"So that's how it's going to be?" Stephen responded with a smile and then he closed his eyes and inhaled deeply. Manny dropped the knife from his hand and reached into his pocket. The moment his hand touched the hilt of the pistol he felt his head spin. All of his senses began to numb and as they returned Manny tried blinking but could only see darkness.

He tried to raise his hands to his head but found his arms tied against his body by a long black chain. He attempted to shout but no sound came out. A numbness went over his body as he now couldn't feel anything. Not the clothes against his skin or the temperature of the room. All that was left was the pressure of the chain wrapped around his body. He could see nothing, feel nothing, smell nothing. Manny wondered if he died in that hallway sitting beneath Stephen. Then from behind him, he began to hear a static droning note from a bass guitar. It gradually grew louder and individual notes were more prominent.

The rhythm was slow and full of emotion as if the player felt the pain of craving love. Now the notes were beginning to vibrate the links and Manny could feel the music in his bones. It hurt. It hurt so much that Manny wanted to scream but he was unable. The rhythm changed to a faster deeper rendition of the same song as before like the source was getting closer.

Then it was just one long note.

Manny couldn't tell how long it lasted. He felt the bones inside his body turn to dust but he was still standing there tied to himself, trying to scream. Before him, a red mist appeared. It swirled around him, vibrating to the note. It floated gracefully in the air falling side to side until it took a feminine form. The fog seemed to have a mind of its own as it began to dance. Manny could imagine a face staring at him with sad gray eyes. His own eyes made their way down to the chest and then to the legs.

Even in pain, the female form gave him a sense of pleasure. Most importantly, it was all red. He had to reach out and touch it. His arm tensed but didn't budge. The mist then multiplied before him and dozens of red mist women were dancing around him to the song being played by the bass. This was torture. He couldn't move. He couldn't act on his impulses to touch the beings in front of him. It was all he wanted.

He started crying, wishing for all of this to end. He didn't even care about Stephen anymore. The thought of going back to that school made him think of being crushed by a boulder or suffocating underground. They weren't his problem and yet he had come out here to save them. For what? They deserved to die.

It was too much. Manny tried to close his eyes and found that he couldn't. If he could speak he'd be wishing for all of this horror to stop. The bass note seemed to be coming from directly behind him now. The mist moved in on him like a harem of red women pressing their soft skin against his body and then he finally felt something touch him.

The headstock of a guitar pressed against his back. Then with great force, it went through his spine and pierced his body. He watched it tear through his chest. The tuners turned as they scraped bone changing the notes of the sound until the strings entered his body as well. The vibrations entered what he imagined was his soul. His vision blurred when he looked down and saw the fretboard protruding from his chest. His blood vibrated to the changing frequencies.

"Wake up!" a voice called out to him. Manny opened his eyes and found himself lying on the hallway floor, screaming. Stephen was kneeling beside him with a hand on his shoulder. "I am sorry," Stephen said. "I am still trying to get the hang of this. You get it, right? I couldn't let you pull the gun out. Those bullets are not for me. I am not your enemy."

"What did you do to me?" Manny asked, clutching his chest feeling his heartbeat. His vision kept slipping between the hall and the red dancers. Hints of melodies crept through his veins.

"I just needed to stop you. I can enter a person's mind and sort of stir their emotions causing them to experience not only their fears but their hopes and dreams all at once. You were only under for about five seconds before you started screaming. That's honestly impressive. Most people freak out immediately. These two did." Stephen motioned to the adults standing behind him. "Try to calm down. Your friends look scared."

The others that came with Manny were gathered around the entrance to the hallway. Manny could see the fear in their eyes. Clearly, knives were not going to win against someone like Stephen. They were speechless. Frozen in fear.

"You can't do that!" Manny yelled at the boy in front of him. "My mind isn't something for you to toy with. You have no right!" Stephen dropped his hand from Manny's shoulder. The look in his eyes turned from concern to discontent. Somehow every action the kid made caused Manny's heart to feel like it was falling inside his chest. "We're people! Stop doing this!" His words echoed through the hall.

"I have to," Stephen said softly. "Try for a second to imagine a life where everyone you trust hurts you. Imagine those you love being so terrified they lock you away and try to pretend you don't exist. Even the best people I've met have abandoned me. I stand beside forgotten souls and guilty flesh. If you could save the world and all the people on it, should you? Have you met anyone you thought deserved to be alive? I'm guessing not. I know I haven't. That was until I met the condemned living plagues behind me. I had to believe there are more people worth saving. This school, my old school, is the perfect setting for an experiment to determine if a large enough of the population can prove that they, at the very least, can earn their lives. I have to do this. I don't want to. If you had the weight of this decision on your shoulders, you'd crumble, like dried blood on the soft faces you love so much. I bear this burden because I refuse to be naive and say everyone should always be saved and I can cast aside my own personal affections. Again, I have to run this experiment even if it means everyone, including us, will die here tonight. My question must be answered. Can you understand this?"

What scared Manny the most, was the sympathy he was beginning to feel for this kid with gray dead eyes. There were plenty of times today that Manny wanted to just let everyone in here die. Leave everyone to suffer. They're doing it to themselves anyway. He looked back at the kids he'd brought with him. When their eyes locked, their faces went from scared to horrified. "You're eyes," Josh stuttered.

Manny looked at Kim. "They're like his," she said as if she couldn't believe she had said the words.

"What?" Manny asked, feeling lost.

"They're silver like Stephen's," the terrified girl replied. Manny reached his hand to his face as if somehow he'd be able to tell if his eyes had changed color. He could feel it already though, not by touch but inside his head. He turned back to Stephen.

"What have you done to me?" he asked. "I am beginning to understand what you're saying. How can you be so sure the world is going to end? How could you possibly save anyone? These questions, I feel I don't need to know the answers. I trust you." The last sentence came out as more of a question than a statement. Where was this coming from? He felt reassured but at the same time filled with doubt. He looked to Stephen.

Stephen smiled at him. His eyes held back a sadness. He felt obligated to help Stephen.

"This experiment must continue," the young boy with silver eyes said to his new friend. Manny watched as Stephen rose from kneeling and walked back into the darkness that he came from. The other two adults followed him, closing the doors behind them.

Manny felt the red mist along the floor flow against his fingers until the last of it entered the hallways behind him.

"Why didn't you stop him?" Kim yelled. Manny looked back at her and wondered why she was so angry. "He was right there in front of you! You have a gun? What was all that about blood and soft faces? Who even are you? Have you been working with him the whole time?" The boys all nodded and voiced their own uncertainty.

The world around Manny seemed to go in and out of focus but his thoughts were clearer than they've ever been. He pulled the pistol from his pocket and aimed at Kim. "What are you doing?" the girl asked. Ben was closest to the hallway. He moved first and scrambled around the corner. Josh and Chris were close behind. Kim did not move. Her eyes were on Manny. He could tell she was holding back tears.

"I don't want to be a part of some test," she said to him in a low shaking voice. "I didn't ask for this. You promised we'd get revenge. You said we'd end this. The way you're looking at me makes me feel this is just beginning. You were supposed to save us."

"I am doing the best I can," Manny said to her, noticing the guilt shake his voice. "I didn't ask you to come with me. I didn't know what we'd find. I don't even understand what's going on. There's a kid that just made me have visions of dying. I died just now. Right here, when I was unconscious. I'm certain of it. He killed me, but as he left my mind he left behind something. It burns. It hurts, but it's like it's cleaning my soul. When I said we'd end this, I meant it. You may not understand but you will. We have to get him to do what he did to me to everyone else."

Manny watched her eyes sink. She was giving up, he thought to himself. She's worthless. Manny lowered the gun. He didn't want to kill her. Her skin wasn't worth bleeding. He stood and went to the door. It didn't budge.

"Stephen!" he screamed while banging on it. "Come back, Stephen! These people need you. If you just do what you did to me, they'll understand." Manny stood back and aimed at the lock. The sound of the gunshot rang throughout the hall. He wasn't expecting it to be so loud. His head rang and the unfocused room spun around his head. He fell back to the floor.

"You were supposed to save us." Kim's voice said through the high pitched squeal traveling in his ears.

"I didn't ask for that responsibility!" he yelled at her. "Anyone in that room could've stepped up! After the classroom, Evrona kept looking at me like I was a monster. Maybe I am, but we're alive and those other kids aren't. She should be thanking me. You should be thanking me." With each sentence, Manny felt himself getting angrier. The clarity he once felt began to fade. He raised the gun at Kim, who was now standing near the exit to the other hall.

"We all just want to go home," she said softly, turning the corner out of sight.

"I thought you wanted to kill Stephen," he shouted after her. Manny stood in the empty hall with the weight of the gun in his hand. The only question he didn't get to ask or get answered was how does this all end?

What could possibly prove to Stephen that the kids in the building were worth saving? Was Manny right this entire time and they are currently being tested? If so, what is the test? The only thing that changed was the red mist flowing through the halls. That can't be a test. Maybe, it's how they deal with surviving, maybe it's whether or not they try to leave, or maybe Stephen has already chosen whose lives are worth saving and wants the worthy to kill off the rest. Would he be so cruel? Manny just needed something, anything, to point him in the right direction. He passed the last test. He would make sure to pass the next. He began to make his way out of the hall.

He barely rounded the corner before the sound of shoes hitting linoleum came from behind him. He turned and saw a woman dressed in black kneeling as if she was trying to be quiet. He looked up and saw the window was open. She came from outside, he realized. This was the first adult he'd seen since this all started besides the ones with Stephen.

She was middle aged with dark brown hair that reminded Manny of woods at dusk. Her appearance made him think of a lawyer or maybe some type of detective. Was this their next test? She was staring ahead at the wall reading one of the posters that were littered about the school.

"Who are you?" he asked, breaking the silence. He watched as fear washed over her. She turned to face him standing upright. She had the same eyes as Stephen. This proved it. She was their next test.

"I'm looking for someone, his name is Stephen-" the woman began to say, but Manny didn't want her to talk. Not yet. He needed to bring her to the lunchroom. The fact that she knows who Stephen is would be enough to prove to the others that he was right. He raised the gun pointing it between her eyes.

"Come with me."

[3: 47 P.M.]

Exalted Endeavors

ASTERIA
October 15, 1999
[3: 47 P.M.]

Asteria Griffin struggled to hold back tears as her captor led her through dark high school halls by her hair. She watched both her shoes and socks slip past a red fog that stained her clothes. The smell of rusted pipes and molding wood consumed her senses.

"Who are you?" the middle aged woman asked the young man. "Where are you taking me? Do you know Stephen? Do you know where he is?"

"How do you know Stephen?" the boy responded, his voice desperate and excited. "You will be able to help us! With you, I'll be able to show the others what I saw."

Their walk was short and hurried. Asteria's pants were wet from water that was pooled on the floor. The boy's steps splashed back at her as well as her own frantic attempts to keep herself upright. Suddenly they stopped and Asteria could see a set of double doors. The boy pushed on one of the doors and it moved a couple inches and then hit something with a loud screech. He took a step back and kicked at the door. Whatever was behind the door fell as metal and plastic crashed together.

"Look, what I've found!" the boy announced to a crowd of frightened teenagers. The sight was unlike anything she'd ever seen.

In all her years of practicing psychology, hosting therapy sessions, and helping people through the worst times in their lives, she had never seen the intense misery that each young face carried. The curious eyes watched as this surprisingly strong young man dragged her to the center of the room and pushed her to her knees.

"This is our next test!" his voice boomed throughout the lunch hall. "Stephen has tested us. It was hard. It was fatal. Those casualties were necessary. I've been tested individually. Ask those cowards in the corner. They witnessed my test, my transformation into a vile human with sick ambitions into a witness of truth. He's using my voice right now to speak to you all. Can you feel it? I know you can. This woman came to us from the outside. The only way that's possible is if she's working with Stephen, or he allowed her to enter. This has to be it."

The lack of confidence in the boy's voice terrified her. Looking around the room the other teenagers seemed uneasy but completely captivated by his words. Were they so lost that they would believe him? Truthfully she could feel her own heart and soul vibrating as if Stephen had manipulated him somehow. She knew all too well the control he could have.

Her eyes were scanning the room hoping to find a hint of silver. This group of battered individuals was the type of destruction she had expected to find in her pursuit to locate the boy. Beside her sat a girl leaning over a boy with a pool of blood. Her hands and arms were stained red. Throughout the crowd, there was fear and tears. What stood behind her was desperation, and he was willing to sacrifice her for his new god.

"Stephen made me face my fears and dreams, my hopes and desires, all at once. Then he killed me. Tell them." The young man raised his gun toward a girl who looked exhausted. The dark rings under her eyes gave it all away.

"What he says is true," she reluctantly said to the crowd. "He's not lying." Her words were quick and precise. A group of boys behind her chimed in and told a tale of confronting Stephen along with two other individuals. It had to be Tuls and Ed, Asteria figured.

"He is here!" she yelled back at the boy. "Take me to him! I can end this."

"Your lies won't work on me," the boy responded. "We have to do to you what Stephen did to me. Tell me, what do you fear? What are your dreams?"

The sudden realization that this boy was intending on killing her in front of all these kids hit her. She felt her face get warm as tears began to swell in her eyes. She spoke in whispers as she began to sob and plead, "don't do this. Where is Stephen?"

"Do you fear what all women fear?" the young man asked, reaching around her head. His fingers slipped around her blouse and he pulled as hard as he could. The soft fabric ripped apart exposing her chest, bra, and stomach. "Do you dream what all women dream?" The cruel boy knelt beside her and caressed her skin.

Asteria's stomach churned from the disgust but she gained her composure. "I know what you are feeling right now. I've felt it too. The ecstasy of his influence radiates from your heart to your mind. It won't last. Those silver eyes you have will fade and you'll end up like me. Empty. The difference between me and the others that this happened to is I didn't kill myself. I'm not afraid to die. That's why I'm trying to find him. So this doesn't happen to anyone else. I'm too late for you. If you stop this, right now. We can save everyone here. Dig deep young man. Find that part of you he left unscathed. We can end-"

When the metal grip of the gun hit her cheek, her voice stopped. She fell over onto the ground and spat out the pooling blood inside her mouth. She looked back at the boy. His mouth was twisted into a smile full of pleasure and excitement. "You're doing this for yourself," Asteria said to him. "Not for Stephen." *I'm going to die here.*

"That's enough Manny!" a girl's voice screamed from beside her. It was the girl who was facing away from her when they first entered the room. She was standing now with blood-stained clothes and a furious look on her face. Finally, Asteria thought to herself, someone with sense. Looking around the room the other kids seemed to want to join this Manny guy. Her voice seemed to halt the bloodlust for now.

"You guys realize this is insane!" the girl screamed out. "We've only been here a few hours and already we're willing to torture and kill a stranger? You've got to be kidding me. Manny, come to your senses. When I first met you you were saving Michelle. Weren't you?" The way the girl was holding herself, Asteria could tell she was exhausted. Her body swayed from side to side and her hair was bundled into a bun that seemed like it could fall apart at any second. The two kids locked eyes. She didn't wait for a response. "I trusted you. I won't let you do this."

The girl looked back at a different girl wearing clothes that were too big for her. The two of them charged at Manny. Asteria went to grab his leg to help subdue him. The boy noticed and quickly turned and kicked her in the face. Everything went dark for a second as she fell back onto the floor.

The sound of fists and grunts being exchanged echoed in her head. Then it went silent.

Through the dizziness, she raised herself to her elbows. The girl who had spoken first was on the ground gripping Manny's pant leg. He was looking down at her like she was a feral dog trying to take him down.

"Everyone," the girl pleaded to the crowd. "Listen to me. We can't let ourselves-" The young man had taken his other leg and kicked her square in the jaw. She fell to the ground unconscious. The other girl ran to her side. Manny stepped beside the girl on the floor and punched her in the side.

"You think this is your moment or something?" he yelled down at her. "Did you think you were going to make a big speech and save the day? We're already dead unless we do what I was shown. Stephen's promised me this. He will kill everyone here unless we pass his stupid tests. There's nothing you can do to stop this. You dumb bitch! I already told you the truth. I can't remember anything before this morning when you found us. I've been honest. And, I'll tell you the truth again. Right now. After her, you're next."

"You're just like him," Asteria said. "You think your ideals are all that matter in the world. That your problems and your issues are for everyone else to care about. You're wrong. Stephen could never accept that. Maybe you can. Outside of these walls is the real world. They'll never understand why you've done these horrible things to everyone here. Not because they're stupid or not worthy, but because what you're doing is insane. After you do what you think Stephen wants you to do, you'll have to leave this school and face the consequences. The police won't forgive you. The parents of these children won't care that you were doing what you thought was right. You will be a murderer. You will go to prison and rot."

Manny had made his way back to her. His shadow was cast on him and in the dark edges, she could see the evil in his eyes. She had to look away. The other kids in the room were waiting anxiously to see how this was going to play out. All their eyes were on them. "Do you really think I'm the end of all of this?" she asked the crowd.

"You're asking the wrong people," Manny's deep voice groaned. He reached down and entangled his fingers in her hair. He raised her body almost entirely off the ground. "Tell me what you fear!" he screamed at her.

"No," she responded. "I won't help you. Not this way."

"Tell me," he said softer. "Please. This won't just help us, but it will help you."

"No, it won't. Stop this and bring me Stephen. I can end this."

"How?"

"If I can find him," Asteria said eagerly. "If you all help me subdue him. I can call my team and they can be here in fifteen minutes. I'll take him and bury him. He'll never see the sun again. He's lost. He needs help. The world isn't ending. He just uses that excuse to use his very special and unique power to manipulate and torture people. I can help him. I can stop this."

The boy released his grip on her hair. The palms of her hands slapped the linoleum as she fell to the floor. Painful tears followed close behind. She looked back at the young man. Her words didn't help.

"Stop," the boy said, tightening his grip on the gun. The next words that came out of his mouth only Asteria could hear. "I died. He brought me back. If he did that to you too then you have to understand. We're all dead without him. You want to know where he is? He was behind the door when you entered the school. Hey, no. You're not going anywhere!"

Asteria had stood and scrambled to run out of the room. Manny pounced on top of her before she could get to her knees. Sitting on her stomach he stared down into her eyes. "What do you fear?" he asked her.

She shook her head holding her emotions back.

"What are your dreams?"

She shook her head again.

"Just tell me so I can help you! I have to remind you."

Asteria began to cry and shield her face in fear.

"Stephen!" the young man screamed out to the crowd. For the first time, he looked around.

Asteria watched him begin to realize no one wanted to be on his side. She could feel the reluctance in the room. No one wanted any of this. They just wanted to go home. The young man's eyes raced across the crowd desperately looking for some form of validation. It didn't exist. He was breathing heavily with unintelligible noises spurting from his lips. After a few moments, he yelled. The sound hurt her ears. Then came the fists.

The first hit her in the side of the head silencing his screaming with a ringing. The second hit her in the chest that caused her to wince in pain. All the air left her lungs. Then the rest came hitting her all over. She could hear the sound of her flesh being pummeled by much rougher hands. Her arms didn't feel real as she tried to shield her face.

It only took a few moments before her bones began to break.

The ones in her arms went first. Then she felt her collar bone move inward which made breathing painful. She couldn't open her eyes but her teeth were piling up in her mouth along with blood and bits of her lip. Then it all just stopped. Where pain should've been, Asteria felt regret.

She could hear blood dripping from his hands onto the floor. He screamed again.

The pressure from her stomach was gone. Through the ringing, she could hear the other kids start to scream. This was immediately followed by the sound of gunshots. Then the sound of bodies hitting the floor. Asteria wasn't sure how many shots were fired or how many kids were hit.

As darkness began to take her, she regretted not being able to stop Stephen. Sure this was Manny, but without Stephen maybe this evil within wouldn't have surfaced so violently. For the first time, she began to hate Stephen.

This blood was his.

[4: 44 P.M.]

The Same Cloth

AUBREY
October 15, 1999
[5: 00 P.M.]

The silence woke Aubrey from her dreams of explosions in the sky. She could remember a red moon being smeared across a deep blue canvas. Brilliant stars pierced through clouds while a crowd on the ground marched to the drone of a bass guitar. Around her, skyscrapers fell into themselves throwing dust into the air. It shimmered as if made of crushed diamonds. As she opened her eyes, the scene twisted unto itself and was replaced by the lunchroom she was hoping was a part of this nightmare.

A few feet away from her lay the woman that Manny dragged here. She was dead. Her face was unrecognizable and smashed in. Even if she was alive, she wouldn't want to be. Aubrey felt someone shove her. She turned her head finding Michelle sitting beside her. She was crying.

"What happened?" Aubrey asked without thinking. She pushed herself from the ground. The strain sent shockwaves of pain throughout her body. She nearly fell back to the ground. Michelle shoved her hands into Aubrey's face. Between her palms rested the large feather she had been carrying with her all day, only it was crumbling into fragments of black ashes that floated off into the air.

"Is that why you're crying?" Aubrey could feel her anger becoming heavy in her throat. The words she wanted to say, the ones that told Michelle she was silly for crying over a feather instead of any of the other tragedies that have happened over the last few hours, froze when she saw the walls painted red. There were other words she wanted to say to the mute, they formed questions about who she was and how she knew Manny. Maybe in some words, she wanted to tell the girl she was done protecting her. All of her rage and curiosity dissipated like a dream she couldn't remember. There was only the red wall.

Just below the wall piled on top of one another were the bodies of her classmates. She counted eight unmoving half clothed young women. Any exposed skin was soaked in a deep maroon. On each of their bodies was a gaping wound of torn skin and flesh. These girls did not die quickly. They suffered and as Aubrey realized this her own blood felt cold. She feared her heart had stopped beating. The carnage reminded her of seeing Michelle for the first time. She turned her head back at the sobbing girl.

Maybe she was crying because this is what Manny had done to her just before Aubrey found them. The image of the blood-soaked crater reminded her of the wall. Many emotions were running through Aubrey right now but the fear of not knowing where Manny was raised above all the others.

"Where is Manny?" Aubrey asked Michelle, feeling the looming presence of the red wall behind her. The girl shook her head and shoved the feather into her face. The trauma made her useless, Aubrey determined.

She could feel her own emotions wanting to surface. The tears would have to wait. They were trapped inside this school with a killer. Even worse, it was a man who seemed to enjoy targeting girls. Sitting in the middle of the empty lunchroom suddenly made Aubrey feel exposed. "Come on." Aubrey pulled Michelle by her hand and the two girls made their way to the hall. *Where did everyone go?*

Out in the hall, not many places came to mind when considering places to hide. There was the front office, the nurse's office, and the hall that led to a separate part of the school. They would check the front offices first.

As they made their way through the hall they were accompanied again by an eerie silence. This time however it seemed there was the sound of running water above them. Examining the ceiling, Aubrey noticed water droplets were beginning to form. The water from the classrooms must have been spilling over throughout the ceiling. No matter what their situation Stephen had placed a time limit. The foam ceiling panels wouldn't last long until the water began spilling into the halls. Could one kid really plan all of this?

The front office was a wall of glass that consisted of many windows and a single door. The windows and the door were lined with wire preventing anyone from breaking in. Aubrey stood in front of the doors staring at all the shattered glass. There were a few bullet holes scattered on the surface. Manny must have tried to get in, Aubrey figured. She tried the door but knew it wouldn't move.

Glass fell to the floor from the shove but the door didn't open. If it was locked that meant there were students inside and they were safe. At least Aubrey hoped this was the case. Michelle grabbed her shirt and tugged. Aubrey turned to face her. Her eyes were red from crying.

The young woman stared at her in the eyes and opened her mouth. For the second time since she first met her, Michelle attempted to speak. Behind her unmoving mouth, Aubrey watched her face turn red and throat tighten from the strain. All she managed was a hum of the beginnings of a word.

"Why now?" Aubrey asked her. "Why are you trying to talk now?" The frustrated girl put her hand to her chest and pounded it. Then she took her other hand and pressed it against Aubrey's chest. She made a motion that seemed to signal a swapping action as she moved her hands back and forth between their chest.

"I'm sorry," Aubrey said to the girl. "I don't understand. We don't have time for this. We have to find Manny or finish Stephen's stupid game." Michelle pushed Aubrey and shook her head. Whether or not what Michelle was trying to say mattered, Aubrey couldn't understand.

"Har…" Michelle managed to get out. The sudden sound of her voice shocked both of them.

In the silence, a low voice crawled around the corner from down the hall.

"I can hear you," the voice said. Aubrey felt chills crawl from the tips of her fingers up her arms through her neck and down her spine. It was Manny. The heavy footsteps of destruction pounded at the linoleum. Aubrey turned and grabbed Michelle's hand and ran.

The lockers rushed past them in a blur of adolescent vaults. If she assumed all the classrooms were locked and full of water then they only had one escape; the windowed hall. The smell of rust and mildew from degraded plumbing and rotting drywall encompassed them. At their pace, the leaks from the ceiling felt like rain.

The two girls stopped at the entrance of their destination. One of the doors was ajar as if someone left it open for them. *Maybe the others went through,* Aubrey hoped.

"You guys are fast." Manny's rough voice caught them off guard. Aubrey was too wrapped up in her head she didn't hear he was chasing after them. She was sure her lungs were frozen. Deep inside her chest, she could feel a heavy breath waiting to be released but knowing this man was behind her it wouldn't come out. The world grew darker. Her head spun.

"What's going on here?" someone from beyond the doors asked. A large man dressed in a buttoned shirt and slacks pushed through the door. He was tall and his heavy voice matched his weight. The hall around Aubrey found its orientation so fast she nearly fell.

All three of the teenagers stood in shock. *A teacher!*

"You have to help us!" Aubrey said, running up to him. The closer she got the hair on her arms and head began to stand straight as if she was about to be struck by lightning. It wouldn't surprise her, not after all she'd been through today. *It hasn't even been a day,* she reminded herself.

She stopped moving and felt her heart begin to ache. She stumbled off to the man's side.

"Nice to see you again," the man said.

"You?" Manny countered.

Aubrey watched the man move down the hall. "Michelle!" she cried out as the mute fell to the floor too.

"I felt this before," Manny said, sounding confused. He was moving back from the man. "Is this you?"

"Stephen sent me," the man responded, ignoring his question. "We don't need you anymore."

The man stepped over Michelle and closed in on Manny. Aubrey could feel her legs again. She tried her arms. It was like her heart was trying to restart the energy within her body. She strained and nearly screamed getting to her hands and knees. She was panting and could hear Manny grunting. It would take too much to look back now.

Aubrey didn't even care what was happening to the boy she once trusted. She stared at the ground watching sweat splash against the water that was pooling all throughout the school. Of all her trials today, this was the hardest. Getting back up. It would've been easier to let the sudden feeling of losing all the energy in her body consume her and go to sleep. Right there in a pool of blood and rust and water. Mostly water.

"Michelle," she said, letting herself breathe. Aubrey pulled herself to the girl. Her eyes were wide and her arms were flinching. This moment felt like earlier in the morning when Aubrey was helping the girl get cleaned up. Michelle was looking at her still unable to speak but her amber eyes were crying out for help.

Aubrey raised herself to her feet. She grabbed the girl by the wrists and began pulling her to the doors. They just needed to get away from the other two. Together.

The water splashed around Michelle with each tug. Just before she reached the double doors Michelle pulled her hands back to her body. Aubrey fell back through the doors.

She looked around in the dark. Light peered between the cracks of the double doors of the windowed hall. The silence seemed to engulf her body. Tendrils of dark silence slipped around her throat. This was the last straw.

"I'm done!" she screamed, scrambling to her feet. The dark seemed to recede and her surroundings materialized as her vision adjusted. She took the opportunity to flex her aching muscles. Not only was this school draining her mind and her heart but now her physical being was being tested.

As she sat in the part of the school she hadn't been yet, two hallways lay before her, one extended directly in front of her and the other sprawled to her left. The walls here had fresher paint and lacked the lockers that were in the other hall. Still trapped. She wasn't sure what she was expecting. Salvation? Sanctuary? She didn't know.

Light poured in as Michelle entered the fork in their road. Their tired eyes met. Against Michelle's damp skin the school's lights a glowing outline appeared around her. Again her beauty stunned Aubrey. The mute girl turned and slammed the door behind her leaving the girls alone in the dark.

"What happened to him?" Aubrey asked. The last she heard only the older man was making noise. Michelle shook her head. "What do you think he meant when he said Stephen didn't need him anymore? Whatever he meant, he didn't seem concerned with us. I bet that's who helped Stephen this whole time. It'd be impossible for a kid to do this alone."

The two girls took a moment to catch their breath and let Michelle's eyes adjust to the dark. The halls looked identical. "Stephen has to be in this part of the school. We're going to end this." Aubrey said the words confidently. She wasn't sure exactly what they meant to her though. *How does this all end?*

"What were you trying to tell me back there?" she asked, finding herself at the threshold of the hall in front of her. Giving no response Michelle walked past her into the abyss.

They walked for a while in an echoed march. The anger that emerged from earlier sat uncomfortably in Aubrey's throat. She found herself wanting to scream. Instead, she kept walking.

"Have you ever seen someone so beautiful?" The words were a whisper but they were clear.

Ahead of them, a door opened and a dim light along with Evrona fell into the hallway. She was holding her dress against her chest but the thick straps meant to hold the clothing in place were ripped. She was crying. The tallest woman Aubrey had ever seen emerged from the doorway.

"You have nowhere to run," the tall lady said down at her. Aubrey and Michelle stopped moving and pressed against the wall hoping they wouldn't see them.

Not only was the woman tall, she had long flowing dirty blonde hair that fell well below her waist. With a long arm, she reached down and grabbed Evrona's dress by its skirt and pulled. Michelle put a hand on Aubrey's shoulder as they watched the struggle.

Evrona kicked and yanked away at the fabric. The blonde used her height to her advantage and heaved so hard they could hear the seams rip and tear. There were piercing sounds of Evrona's skin smearing against the linoleum alongside a flurry of curses and screams. "Let go of me you sadistic bitch! My dress! You fucker! You fucking slut witch!" Both women vanished into the room. The door slammed behind them.

"How many accomplices do you think Stephen has?" Aubrey asked aloud. "If they're all trapping the kids that enter this side of the school there has to be an exit." She looked at Michelle and she nodded.

They began to move down the hall this time being mindful of the noise they were making. Stopping just before where Evrona was lying they waited and listened. Many different voices could be heard inside. Although they were muffled Aubrey could hear the blonde woman's voice the loudest.

"Is this the first time you've seen a woman naked?" she teased. "Take it in. I'm not ashamed. This could be your only chance. I've got my orders and while the pillow boy contemplates the results of his tests I'll have some fun of my own. We've been watching you guys the whole time. Sure you've all made choices but why didn't any of you make the right ones? Oh well. I don't care. I'm here for him. Not you. Don't look at my scars!"

The last sentence was wailed with such anger and sadness Aubrey felt like it was her own mother yelling. It was one of those yells where you're doing something wrong and your parent out of disappointment and shock yells a little too loud.

Michelle shoved her. She must've noticed. Aubrey kept moving.

With each step, the weight of guilt became heavier. What was she supposed to do? Try to stop that woman? She was clearly bigger and stronger than all the kids in the school. Even if they all simultaneously attacked her, which she knew wouldn't happen, Aubrey was sure the woman would overpower them.

It would be better if she managed to get out and find help. Why risk being caught herself? She had to escape. Police were more helpful than some teenage girls. The guilt only grew. She kept thinking of the look on Evrona's face and the fear in Manny's voice.

Michelle's soft fingers slipped into her palm. The guilt remained.

In front of them two large doors emerged from the darkness. A sliver of light crept through the distance between them. This time without hesitation both girls put their hands on the push mechanisms and walked through together.

Their eyes adjusted to the bright light Aubrey kept hoping they were outside. She was greeted with a view of the school's gymnasium. There were multiple basketball courts, off to the side sat a set of bleachers, and on the other side a small stage. The walls were tall and adorned with school trophies and posters and athletic awards. To the left of the stage stood two doors marked for locker rooms, one boys and one girls. Past that was another set of double doors with a bright red neon sign with the word EXIT above it. Whether or not the word held any truth was unknown. There was a hum from the large tube lighting that hung from the ceiling. Above the bleachers were small windows well over ten feet from the highest seat. Most importantly, there was light coming through those windows and Aubrey saw the sky for the first time since the morning. A gradient of blue to gray like a well worn set of dark blue jeans. The light from outside hit the middle of the gym and marked the spot where a young man was standing. He was talking to himself.

"What if I'm wrong?" he muttered, over and over.

[5: 21 P.M.]

Conversions of the Sky

MANNY
June 16, 2012
[11: 52 A.M.]

    The hum of the tires against asphalt vibrated the old green car. It was like a long low note that droned and strained to keep going as he pulled to a stop at a red light. Beside him was a park as vibrant as spring and alive as summer. The sound of kids screaming and pedestrians talking and laughing replaced his lonely note. He looked out at the lush scenery.

    The sun was shining down on all the people despite a few stray clouds attempting to ruin the day. A couple was walking with their dog smiling as if they were happy. The small white goldendoodle even seemed cheerful as it pranced ahead of them. Further behind them stood a playground. All Manny could make out was a blur of bright yellows, greens, blues, and reds, as kids ran around their parents and each other. Next to the playground an ornate and lavish fountain ejected water into the air and received it just as some engineer designed it to. A dozen or so people stood around admiring it. Love-struck teenagers sat on the rim and pretended to be in love while holding hands. As much as the scene frustrated Manny, it was a nice day so he tried to not let it bother him.

    Taking a deep breath, Manny looked to the sky and watched the clouds lazily drift through the blue canvas. On the East side of the park, three large skyscrapers reached for the sun. Below them, a few office and apartment buildings littered the space. A half dozen parking garages obstructed what would otherwise be a beautiful view from the street.

"The world has been judged! We are not worthy!" A cacophony of voices danced from the middle of the park out into the city. They were all chanting the phrase over and over. Manny looked for the source and spotted a crowd coming from the main street spilling out into the park. Hundreds of men, women, teenagers, and children blocked the streets in front of him. The cars behind him blared their horns. The light was green but with all the people Manny couldn't move his car.

"Where do you want me to go?" he yelled, rolling down his window. Before he knew it, a large man stood beside his door.

"What's this all about?" he shouted at the kids marching. "I've got a meeting!" The man was dressed as if he thought he was important. Black suit, collared shirt, and black pants all ironed of course. The sweat rolling down his forehead either hinted at the man's anger or the overwhelming heat the day had to offer.

"They're here to save the city." One of the kids took a moment from their chanting to respond to the man. It was a girl with mahogany hair and black lipstick. Her skin reminded Manny of black licorice, the way it glistened in the light and was just as dark.

Something about the way she said the word 'save' compelled Manny to open his car door and join the caravan of drivers surrounding his car. He wanted to talk to the girl. Maybe ask if she liked music. For a brief moment, they locked eyes and he became fully aware of how he looked.

His dirty clothes were just a little too big for him. He'd lost weight since coming back from overseas and only had a handful of clothes that fit right. His short brown hair was oily and his skin felt grimy. *When was the last time he showered?* He couldn't say for certain. What he did know was he wasn't worth a second glance from a girl like her. The shirt she wore had some band he'd never heard of but she must have cut the neck because it rested on one shoulder and fell below the other. It exposed the red strap of a bra that dug into her thin shoulder. Her ripped purple skinny jeans traced the outlines of her panties making Manny wonder if the color matched. She was across the street when she faded into the crowd.

Although he knew he'd probably never see her again Manny lingered on the thin red line that flowed down to her chest. He could paint her. She already liked red.

He did too.

"Get back in your car, man," the man in the suit shouted. "They're all gone." A few kids trotted across the street as if they were scared of being left behind. The man was already standing by his car with the door open. Manny shouted some indistinct confirmation at him and went for his own door. He sat for a moment with it open listening. A voice, strong and confident was being projected from the middle of the park. The sudden shriek from the car horn behind him subdued his curiosity.

The hum of the tires against the road filled his car again as he drove down the street beside the park. He stole glances at the crowd wondering what was going on. In the passenger seat sat a bag of women's clothing. He wasn't sure if Holly would like it but it came from her closet. This was the first step to letting her work for him.

For the past week, she had been allowed to be on the main floor with a chain, of course. She needed to regain her strength and clean herself up before getting back out into the real world. Having a roommate wasn't something new to Manny, during college he and Mikal lived together. Back in those days whenever Holly was in their home, she wore clothes around him, now she wore chains. It would be hard letting her go, but she'd served him well and she promised more girls. More blank canvases. A feeling of anticipation roared inside of him. He needed to get home.

A loud crack interrupted his thoughts. It came from the direction of the park. The sky was different. It was crimson as if hours passed in an instant. Two long streaks of smoke split the sky into different pieces. The top part of the second largest building was leaning. A rumbling filled the park as stone and wood cracked and splintered. Then it fell over and onto itself. One of the smoke trails ended where the building was crumbling. The other missed all the architecture and Manny saw the object it followed just before it slammed into the ground. The object made contact with some of the teenagers that were in the crowd. Their flesh ripped from their bones and disintegrated from the heat. Their blood burst into a red mist. He slammed on his brakes in time with the explosion of dirt and screams.

Dust was filling the streets. The soldier in Manny reacted first. He took a deep breath and exited his car heading for the impact site. The park was in chaos. Children were crying and mothers and fathers were screaming. As he got closer to the hole in the ground he ran through a blood mist that left trails of blood and sweat streaming down his face. Surrounding the crater was a mound of dirt and a few half-torn bodies laying about. There was no saving them, they were already gone.

Manny peered into the hole trying to get a look at whatever it was that fell from the sky. Through the dust and blood, Manny started coughing. It was getting harder to breathe. At the bottom of the pit, the body of a woman lay alone and completely bare. She had a bloodied chest but seemed to be breathing. In all the chaos, he could get her home without anyone noticing…

"Is she okay?" It was the man in the suit. He was standing beside Manny looking into the hole in the ground as well.

"I don't know," Manny said as he chased his previous thoughts from his head. A teenager was standing on the other side of the crater looking down at the girl. Manny was out of breath from running but he leaped into the hole. Someone needed to help her.

The climb down was easy enough. The dirt was solid besides the fresh blood that painted its walls. As he got closer he looked for whatever it was that hit the ground and the girl. If it hit her it would have killed her, he told himself. He reached the bottom of the hole and knelt down beside her. The ground was almost too hot to touch. Whatever fell to the Earth could be buried in the dirt. He put his finger below the girl's nose. He felt her exhale. Somehow in her state, she was alive.

"Hey," he shouted out. "She's alive!" He looked above trying to find the teenager or the man. His eyes met the teenager's.

A sudden silence fell onto Manny and the girl. The teenager mouthed the words *I'm sorry*. A flash of light emerged from the boy's chest and fell onto the crater. It consumed the ground and them both. It blinded Manny for a moment. He blinked and he was staring up at a clear night sky. A bit of dust hung in the air.

The air around him was cold like an autumn morning. "Hello?" a young female voice shouted down at them.

[7: 03 A.M.]

Ataraxy

AUBREY
October 15, 1999
[5: 21 P.M.]

Aubrey's eyes felt heavy as she stood watching the young man she'd been afraid of all day. She and Michelle were only a foot away from him. His hands were pressed to either side of his head as if he had a migraine. He was hunched over. Both legs were shaking. He was afraid.

"What if I'm wrong?" The sentence filled the room casting doubt on the walls and the light.

"Wrong about what?" Aubrey asked. Her throat felt hoarse. Stephen didn't respond. Her question was ignored. She knew he could hear her. She watched his eyes glance at her and then back at nothing.

A wave of anger awakened inside. It traveled from the bottom of her chest into every muscle in her body. She clenched her fist and teeth and squeezed her eyes so hard tears fell down her face. Her body ached. Michelle must've noticed because her thin fingers slipped around her shoulder. Aubrey pulled her arm away. She stepped up next to Stephen.

"Why are you afraid?" she asked him. Her voice was shaking. Stephen stopped muttering and looked at her. "What if you're wrong? Wrong about what?"

"I've watched my best friend be taken from me," he said softly. "I've been tortured. The strongest man I've ever known was consumed by his own wrath. All I have are ashes and his fire. When humanity found beings stronger than themselves, they hid them in vaults that were never meant to be opened. The rooms behind locks with no keys were home to souls that didn't know they were damned. Under the guise of mental health treatments, we were bound and gagged and forgotten. Asteria told us she would help us. We don't need help. We are the helpers. I was given the future, humanity's future. I'm left with this in one hand the flames of my friend, in the other, the fate of those who don't even know I exist and I've been asked to choose. Are innocent lives worth saving if it means humanity is left to prosper? What would you do? Let a cruel unforgiving species continue to destroy, steal, rape, pillage, all in ignorance? Does the worst of our nature dictate the rest? I have to choose.

"If I decide we deserve a second chance, I am responsible for the consequences. Every death at the hands of a human is on me. Every injustice, theft, or murder, that blood is on my hands. A mother suffering because she loses her daughter to a car crash, a son committing suicide because his father relentlessly beats him, or a junkie overdosing from their preferred drug, if I choose we get a second chance then those happen because of me. Because of me. My choice allows evil to exist.

"People are the only animals capable of evil. Did you know that? We can find evidence of human traits throughout the animal kingdom. Laughter, companionship, love, they're all there, but not evil. We're the ones that are able to recognize that our actions can either be good or bad.

"That's where this school comes into play. Admittedly, choices in the world are too obscure, too vague. Is it good or bad to go to work every day of your life? If you are lazy, are you evil? What about the motivational speaker that cheats on his wife, or the nun that cuts herself for her past sins? It wasn't meant to be clear, but what if I created scenarios where the choices were just that. I introduce a test to a lunchroom full of kids consumed with all their own problems and thoughts. A crown, sure it's a beautiful crown, but a piece of metal with no hidden meaning. If everyone ignored it then I could deduce a relatively large population is capable of choosing not to act on their greed. Simple, or so I thought.

"You all fail. So I get to thinking that maybe it was too broad of a question, too ambiguous. My next step is to make the tests and their choices precise. Segregate the students into classrooms and let them know they are being tested. My assumption here is that the majority of the tests will pass and the losers, well they didn't deserve to live anyways, right? Once the water settles, I tally the results. Half of the rooms pass and the other half fail. Impossible. Unless… unless that was the point.

"I've simultaneously solved both of my problems. The evil ones that could not pass the test no longer exist. I hold no responsibility for their actions because they already made their choice. I am left with the good in humanity that made the right choice. This has to be my answer, the only conclusion. Remove the evil from the world and preserve the good. It can be that simple. I don't need to make the decision since the answer is obvious. Or… I was meant to interpret this all differently. What if I'm intended to believe that there is good in the world? I'd find any excuse to save it, save anyone. Then my decision could be unreliable. It has to mean something and again I'm left with a choice. I have to choose. What if I'm wrong?"

"Stop," Aubrey interrupted him. "Just stop." She couldn't bear it anymore. The weight of the words the boy said was just too exhausting. Her head hurt, there was a tightness in her chest, and she could barely focus on what he was saying. "It doesn't matter. This is ridiculous. You can't save the world. You've just tortured a bunch of teenagers, Stephen. All of this to make yourself feel better? I wouldn't trust you to make any decision for me."

The look on his face was the same as her mother's. It said, no one cares how you feel. It's already been decided. This didn't help hinder her anger. In fact, it made it worse.

"You are the girl," Stephen said, saving himself from a slap. He wasn't looking at Aubrey. "You are *his* girl. I watched the two of you dance in the sky as you fell from your sanctuary. I can feel it; your strength."

Stephen reached out to Michelle. Aubrey was too confused to know what to do. The girl she'd been with all day reached out to him. They interlocked hands and the two of them looked at peace, rejuvenated even. In a fit of rage, Aubrey swung her arm between them, breaking their connection. "I'm tired of feeling like a piece in a game where I don't know the rules!" she yelled. "Do you know her?"

"If by that you mean have we ever met, then no," Stephen replied. Somehow through the tone of his voice, his words comforted her. A part of her felt like letting go. It would be easier than fighting him.

"Heart," Michelle said. Aubrey's blood turned cold. She spoke. The girl she'd begged to talk to her spoke to Stephen. Not to her. She was looking into his eyes like a long-lost friend finally visiting after years of being gone. She could feel her blood pulsing in her veins.

"What?" Aubrey said in disbelief. She took a step back from the two of them. Michelle put her hands together and then apart. It was the same way she had done earlier in the hall. Stephen nodded his head with excitement like a kid being told he could have his favorite toy.

"That's right!" he exclaimed. She could hear it in his voice. Stuck in his throat were so many words left unsaid. The two of them interlocked their hands again and embraced each other in an intimate hug. Aubrey took another step back.

"I will get you back to him," Stephen continued, overcoming his joy. "I never thought I'd actually meet you. Only in visions have I seen your eyes. You never had a name so I called you Alice. You aren't supposed to be here and I can get you back to him. This is it. You are my answer. I will save the world."

Stephen squeezed the girl into his chest. He was crying. Michelle was holding onto the crumpled feather she cherished. Her grip was crushing the edges.

"That's great for you guys!" Aubrey screamed. "I'm glad you've got it all figured out. Was it worth it? Was terrorizing me worth it to you? Were the lives of the kids here a price to pay for your feelings? Was Manny a part of this too? I don't even care. I just want to go home!"

The sound of a slamming door consumed the room. All three of them looked toward where Aubrey and Michelle had walked in. The tall blonde that dragged Evrona into the classroom and the large man that was fighting with Manny were standing at the threshold. Each of them was holding onto Manny. He was unconscious. Atop his head was a large red spot that was dripping onto his clothes and the floor.

"What's going on?" the tall woman asked Stephen. "I thought the only one we had to capture was this one?" Her voice hurt Aubrey's ears.

"Aubrey," Stephen said, ignoring the blonde. "Hey, everything is okay. What would you do if I asked you to save the world in a decade? Do you think all of this was easy? I've sacrificed. I'm sorry. That's not what I mean. Were our lives worth less than those kids? I'd argue not. Either way, we were locked inside cages with no intention of opening them. I understand that you feel all life is precious. The truth is I can't save everyone anyways. I can save you though. I will tell you anything you want. Just calm down."

"Piece," Michelle said to Stephen.

"I know," he responded. "You want to know the truth. Manny is not working for me. Sure, I was in the process of converting him to our ways, but he was doing it all wrong. This man, the one they're holding, he's sick. I was trying to help him. He resisted. I need him. You are okay. You will get to go home. That's what you want, right?"

Aubrey looked at Michelle. She felt trapped. Stephen was in front of her and his friends were behind her. She couldn't focus on his words. Her chest was tight and felt empty. Michelle betrayed her. That hurt the worst. They spent the whole day together. She trusted her. Protected her. This entire time, she should have been taking care of herself. Saving herself.

A light was coming from Aubrey's hands. It was spreading over her body. She was the last one to notice. It was warm, like waking up on a cold Sunday morning with two or three blankets all over. All the fear and confusion disappeared from her heart. She was calm.

"Pieces of heart," Michelle said. The girl stepped up to Aubrey, put her fists together, and then took them apart. A smile spread across her face. She put her fists back together. Aubrey still didn't understand what it meant but that was okay. Her entire body was engulfed in an amber glow.

"She is protect," the girl said to Stephen. He nodded understanding what she meant.

"No!" Manny's voice boomed. Aubrey turned in time to see him punch the blonde in the face. Her thin body fell to the floor. The sound of her bones hitting each other made Aubrey feel uneasy. Before the man beside him could react Manny lunged at him. She heard his fists hit the man's face. As if he'd done it a million times before, Manny jumped off the man and directed his foot into the side of his head. During the exchange, the man had grunted a few times but now he lay on the floor unmoving and silent.

"I thought you were going to choose me!" Manny ran at the three of them. The light around her body made her feel safe. She watched Manny run past her and grab Stephen. The look of horror fell on his face as Manny slammed his head into the kid's. "Take it back!" Manny yelled.

"What are you talking about?" Stephen responded. She could hear the fear in his voice. She felt calm.

"I thought if I passed the tests then I would become one of you guys," Manny said. "My eyes are the same as yours. I was supposed to be yours, not her! Take whatever you gave her back. It's mine. I earned it. Give it to me." Manny pushed Stephen to the ground. His attention went to Michelle. He wrapped his arm around her neck. "Do it or I'll kill her."

"Don't," Stephen said from the floor. This was the last word that was said in the room.

Manny, Stephen, and Michelle watched Aubrey as the surrounding light retracted to her chest. The only thought in her mind was to save everyone from Manny. Stephen sprang to his feet and threw himself over the other two. All the light in the room bent toward Aubrey's body.

Helplessly, they watched as the room fell into darkness, except for a condensed orb in front of Aubrey's chest. The roar of a tornado seemed to blare from the same spot. The collected light emanated onto Stephen. It made contact with his clothes shredding them to lint and embers as it burned through like a magnifying glass against a piece of paper. The ray of light continued onto his body, charing a large scar in the shape of the number three on his back. His flesh ignited and burned so quickly that it turned to embers and floated away as ashes. From head to toe, the ray emitting from Aubrey's chest tore Stephen's body apart cell by cell leaving a cloud of ashes where he once stood.

Then Aubrey watched as the surrounding room exploded into rubble. Plumes of smoke and dust engulfed her. The air around her twirled around her body like a cyclone of rubble and ashes. The walls fell over crumbling into gravel that were thrown out into the cold day. Michelle and Manny were lifted from the ground and thrown into the air. Each of them mixed into the clouds and were lost to Aubrey as a veil of light surrounded her burning anything that got close to her.

She looked up to the sky. The sun was setting.

[6: 42 P.M.]

Bed of Fire

MANNY
October 15, 1999
[6:47 P.M.]

When he awoke, Manny found himself lying in a stream with water flowing around him. On one side was a small ridge that declined towards the water. A line of trees stood at the top. Leaves blanketed the forest floor. The water was cold but felt good against his skin. Along the water's edge, dirt, rocks, and sticks contoured the path. On the other side, a forest of the same type of trees blurred into the night. Half of his body was out of the water. With great effort, he turned over and crawled to the shore. His weak arms folded, he fell to the side and rolled onto his back. The sky above was a gradient of blues and grays and oranges. The clouds were red and pink like cotton candy. The sound of Stephen screaming in pain resonated in his mind.

The sky gave no answers to what he just witnessed. His breathing was heavy. He thought for sure he and Michelle were going to die. The scene played again in his head. Aubrey rising from the ground. Her body glowing a vibrant red then consuming all the light. The ray of light that was meant for him. Stephen taking the hit. Then suddenly the world was spinning around him until it just stopped. He was left with mud in his mouth. He was alone in this ditch, sore and cold. The air was brisk enough that he could see his breath. If it weren't for the screams and yelling, he would be tempted to go to sleep.

Over the ridge, the students were pouring out of what used to be the gym. The roof no longer hung over the area. Most of the walls had crumbled in the explosion. Concrete pieces and charred wood littered the perimeter. Beyond them, the kids from the school sat in the damp grass. Some of them were crying, some were screaming, but most of them watched the fire spread from the gym onto the rest of the building. Sitting in the parking lot was a single car, the engine sputtering as it struggled to siphon the last bit of fuel from its tank. The building burned beside a forest and a long country road. In the distance, a small town peered just above the horizon. The opposite direction didn't offer much, just a couple of houses and a large farm.

Manny regained his energy. The fire and smoke stretched into the twilight, standing as a beacon calling for help. Someone in the town down the road would notice it. He pushed himself onto his feet and jumped up to the solid ground. The scenes of chaos settled onto him.

Through the fire, the dust, the tears, and the blood, Michelle sat at the center. She was on her knees, folded onto herself as if in pain. Standing beside her, Aubrey watched. The remaining kids left the building. Her eyes were on Michelle in her silence. They were standing in the same spot as if the room hadn't blown up.

The short walk across the lawn took more energy than he anticipated. He walked past all the kids he'd met during the day. None of them witnessed the worst of his actions. The red wall would be gone by the time anyone came to save them. The mound of bodies below it would be reduced to ashes. Even the water from the stream washed away all the blood from his skin and clothes. He caught Drake glaring at him.

The boy comforted a girl Manny didn't recognize. He was looking at him as if this was all his fault. Every student shared the responsibility for this outcome. Stephen may have set them in motion, but it was their choice to suffer together. For once, his hands weren't the only ones with blood on them. Drake must not have felt the same way. He shook his head, bringing his attention back to those around him. They sat around him as if he'd saved them all. It wasn't him, Manny wanted to shout. It was Aubrey.

He reached the edge of the ruined school. Evrona stood beside a support beam, watching the two girls in the middle. Her makeup was a mess and her clothes were ripped and torn. Dried tears mixed with eyeliner ran down her face. "What were you crying about?" he asked her.

"Nothing," she responded. "What are they doing?"

"Nothing." Manny chuckled. "My guess is they're in shock. Aubrey did something. I'm not sure what, but you can see what happened. She killed him. The one responsible for trapping us in the school. I can't explain it. There was a flash of light and I woke up back there in the water. It was her."

Evrona looked at him, confused. He shrugged. Even if he understood what happened, he didn't know how to explain it. "There were five of us in that gym. I watched that boy's body disintegrate as if she tore him apart atom by atom. He turned to dust. Right in front of me. I need it. That power."

"For what?" she asked him. "What are you even talking about? What power?"

Manny shook his head. It would be pointless to answer her. He stepped onto the hardwood floors. The sound of rocks against wood crunched beneath his boots. Evrona was left among the rubble, more confused now than at any other moment in her life. The air got warmer the closer he got to the two girls.

The smell of iron and insulation washed over him. Aubrey was standing with her head looking up at the twilight sky. It was as if the air surrounding her sat still. Suspended in awe. Manny could see pieces of the building float in place all around her. She looked frozen in time. Michelle was curled up beside her, resting on her knees. Her back appeared to strain to stay down. Every second or so, her clothes would rise off her body like a gust of wind came from below her.

"Aubrey," Manny said. "Let me help you." He reached out for her.

Before he could touch her, Michelle yelled at him.

"Get back!" she said. Her voice was rough and barely above a whisper, but she yelled it again.

Michelle's arms were thrown out from under her. What looked like black flames engulfed her body and shot out in all directions. Sparks of darkness flashed all around them. Tendrils of a black ooze sprang from the flames, reaching for anything it could find. The fire spread into the sky, canopying the school grounds. The stars faded into black, along with the trees and lights from the town down the road. All the streetlamps disappeared when the dome of darkness fell onto it. At the center of it all, Michelle had her hands engrossed in the flames and slime and dark. It resembled what Manny imagined a leak from an industrial oil well would look like, from the desperation in her face to clog it to the uncaring, relentless stream coming from the earth. From what Manny could tell, they were entrapped in this dome of darkness. If it weren't for Michelle's efforts, it would be worse. Manny didn't know how he knew it, but he had a feeling if she wasn't trying to suppress it, the flames would consume the world. Then the kids began to scream.

All around them, kids were crying and screaming. Some of them were calling for help, others were talking to people that weren't there, and some were frozen like Aubrey. Dread replaced relief. Manny could see the black chains and ooze on all the kids. This is what happened to him earlier inside the school, he suddenly realized. This was Stephen. He could feel him on his skin, in his heart, and in his head. The world began to spin.

The cries of suffering balanced Manny. His vision almost went dark, but the surrounding carnage shocked him awake. He stumbled back. Evrona's voice rose above all the others. He scanned the crowd and found her.

She was standing above Drake, stomping on his head. Her blood soaked legs were consumed in the black fire. Beside her, a pair of kids were chasing a different teenager with knives he had passed out earlier. The strain to keep his focus gave him a migraine. "Hey, Manny." The voice came from Michelle's direction.

"Holly?" he responded, dumbfounded. All at once, the world steadied, and he felt alert. Standing in front of him stood the first girl he kidnapped. That's right, he thought to himself, I have kidnapped people. Some events of taking her flashed before his eyes. The sun was bright that morning.

"Yeah," she said. "It's me." She looked just the way he had left her in his basement, naked and chained. This time, the chains were black, and they wrapped around nearly every inch of her body. The chains themselves looked to be consumed in fire. Her pale skin peeked through the links, beckoning him.

"Why are you here?" he asked. His legs felt weak.

"You tell me." She smiled. "You're the one whose mind is being consumed by madness. Why did you think of me?"

"I didn't even remember you until I heard your voice. Wasn't I going back to you? Then something fell from the sky. People died. Wait, if I'm here, then what happened to you? It's been at least a day."

"Don't lie to me," she responded with disappointment in her voice. "You know what happened to me. I'm still there in that house with that other girl. You don't belong here, not in this place and not in this time. Neither does she." Holly stepped up to Manny. She was shorter than he was by nearly half a foot. Her brown hair seemed to float around her head as she walked. The dirt marks on her face outlined her features that he had forgotten.

When she was close enough to touch, she stopped. She extended her arm, the black chain unraveled, and she threw it around his neck. It snapped as she yanked it down. Their eyes were level. He could feel the warmth from her breath as she spoke. "This is what would have happened the moment you let me free."

The links clinked together as the chain tightened around his throat. "Fires burn for the same reason we hear music in nothing. Songs can be heard where none exist. It's always there, like the bass hidden behind melodies. It's the guilt in the bliss. The price for being evil."

Michelle let out one last exhausted scream. The flames and chains flew back to the source. The darkness retracted back toward the palms of her hand. Holly smiled at Manny as the chains that were around his neck were pulled back into the fire. As suddenly as it was cast upon them, the darkness was gone. What remained was a small flame suspended in Michelle's palms. The sky returned along with the calm silence.

"I've got him," the once mute girl said with relief in her voice.

Manny was left with the feeling of abandonment. The apparition of Holly was the only sense of belonging he'd felt since arriving at the school. He wondered if Michelle felt the same. This loneliness brought from displacement. The image of her falling to Earth entered his mind. Not of earth, not from now. She didn't belong even more than him. His throat was sore.

"A black fire," she said to no one in particular.

The other teenagers were left stunned and confused. Those that survived the dark were more terrified than when they were trapped in the school. The realization that they were capable of great evil just like everyone else was tough to swallow.

"His fire was strong," she continued. "More concentrated. Desperate for escape."

Back to normal, Aubrey sat on the ground in fear, covered in dust. Her eyes were on the flame dancing in Michelle's hands. "What are you?"

The sound of her voice reminded him that she killed Stephen. Where there was once a connection between his soul and all the others Stephen had infected, there was nothing but anger. It wasn't just the fact that he didn't belong here that made him feel so alone. It was Aubrey's fault as well. She took away the only connection he had made. Stephen made him feel like he had a reason for being here. He was gone, and so was his purpose. A call for action vibrated inside him. All those who were once connected were begging him to right the wrong. Justice must be delivered.

Aubrey's fist hit his face just as a blood vessel burst in her left eye. Manny was staring down at her with his hands wrapped around her throat. He must have been moving while thinking his previous thoughts. He didn't belong to himself. His new purpose would be to live for those Aubrey stole from. He squeezed harder, feeling the cartilage inside grind and scrape together. Just before her eyes rolled to the back of her head, her skin began to glow.

His hands burned, but he persisted. One last snap turned her cold. A victory shared amongst friends he never met. Satisfied, he stepped off of her. Michelle had watched the whole thing.

"Why?" she asked.

"I had to," he responded. "For everyone."

"She will come back," she said. "Not as herself, but again. You felt her flame leave her body?" She was struggling to speak through her damaged vocal cords.

"Is that what that was? Who are you? What is in your hands?"

"I was made for this," she said with melancholy in her voice.

Beyond the road, the faint sound of sirens could be heard coming from the town. Carefully, Michelle walked through the ruins and out into the forest. Manny followed her through the dark. What would he even say to any authority, he wondered. There were no words that could explain why he was there or why he did what he did. For now, he knew he needed to be with Michelle.

He needed answers.

[7: 02 P.M.]

Salvation in Ignorance

RONALD
October 15, 1999
[9:16 P.M.]

Ronald watched the paramedics as they spoke to the kids. The light from their trucks and floodlights made the area feel exposed. Lines of charred grass, blood splatters, and footsteps covered the lawn on this cold autumn night. Where once a school had stood, only coals and crumbled stone remained. There was no doubt in his mind that one of the Castle creatures had been here.

"Is this a new unit?" His partner Kip asked the question. This was their fifth assignment together, and he was beginning to get more confident in his position. *We are the facade between castles...* Ronald began to recite the oath they both took in his head. It calmed him.

"No," he responded. "They're just not used to this." In the history of Castle, this was the most public incident. Multiple casualties, kids and adults, and one of their own were left for them to find. *Was this Stephen?* He couldn't be sure. A part of him hoped it was, and for good reasons. The first was that he finally left them a trail to follow, and the second he didn't want to think about. If this was something or someone new that they didn't know, this was going to get a lot worse. This could be the end of Castle.

"They were trained for this exact thing, man." Kip took his walkie from his hip and rattled off orders. Ron hoped someone was listening to his passionate speech. His attention was on capturing the details of the landscape before they rebuilt it. They had a two-hour window from when they arrived to gather all the information they could. Everything was important. Asteria's car was off, but the hood was still warm.

Inside the car was a folder with all the information she had collected on Stephen over the last few years. A corner of a handwritten journal entry stuck out the top. He had heard the power those pages possessed. Better to leave it alone, he thought to himself. *Protect your mind.* The glove box concealed a pair of sunglasses and her assigned firearm. It was only a couple of days since he had handed it to her. He could still remember the circles around her eyes. The dark, war torn face accentuated her eyes. A gift from Stephen, stunning silver eyes. It was hard to believe she was gone.

Nothing else in the car was worth taking besides the folder. Asteria's legacy. Leaving the car behind, he made his way toward the school. Kip was directing a group of medics away from the area. His focus was on cleanup. They all knew their job became more difficult the longer they were on the premises.

They were lucky this occurred at night, as lucky as one can be when a nuke goes off in your backyard. The way Ron saw it, either Kip helped clear the scene or he would try to help investigate. Kip was a good agent, but his amateur skills tend to get in the way. Ron has been tracking these creatures for nearly his whole life. While this situation was far from ordinary, remnants of their presence remained. The fire, destruction, and death were obvious.

An inexperienced hunter would miss the fluctuation of temperature in the air, the feeling of dread in their soul, or the perfectly clean areas that were surrounded by chaos. Ron found such a spot at the center of the gym. A circle untouched by the dust. Aubrey Hammond was found here, dead. *Murdered.* A student, unremarkable. *What did it mean?* From the center of the gym, he could see out past the lawn to the dense forest that sat behind and beside the school.

"Did you want to be there for the interviews?" Kip asked as he approached Ron. Something about the trees seemed wrong. There just wasn't enough time to do everything.

"No," he responded. "Get started without me. Take notes. I'm going to take a walk through the school."

"Sure, boss. What are you hoping to find?"

"I'm not sure." He told the truth of it. Something about the area felt different from all the assignments he had worked on. Without taking the entire night in, he wouldn't find any answers.

"Alright," Kip responded. "I'll get started then."

Ron watched him walk across the gym floor. His partner wasn't getting the same feeling he was; the overwhelming doubt. The fire had spread over the roof of the school but a pool of water was in the rafters and subdued most of the blaze.

The door to the main part of the building looked like it wouldn't last till morning. The doors were bent and broken, barely hanging onto their hinges. Water flowed from the inside even though they turned off the main water from the outside. Inside, the halls were filled with smoke and rubble. The fire was mostly put out at this point. Embers littered the ruins, along with the sound of crackling charcoal. He walked through the wide corridors, taking in the remnants of the night. In one room, burnt clothes were strewn about, he wondered why anyone would be compelled to remove their clothes in a burning building.

Traversing the landscape, Ron took note of the blood on the walls and floor, the bullet casings left behind, and the tight seals on half of the classrooms. The atmosphere inside the ruins was the same as Pandora. Those walls were made mostly of wood, unlike the school, whose walls were made of cement. What burned in the fire was the roof, which caused the walls to shift and sway and crumble without support. That and whatever caused the explosion in the gym almost caused the entire building to fall.

Standing where the front offices once stood, he could smell death. He'd have to tell the recovery unit to double check this area. These creatures are okay leaving the dead behind, but not Castle. *Everyone deserves to be put to rest.* The lunchroom was interesting. From what he could tell, it was a temporary sanctuary. There was a stockpile of food and water in one corner, along with some jackets and book bags. This must have been where they met when they realized they were trapped. It was the wall of dried blood with the burnt remains of teenagers that disturbed him. *Was this Stephen? Was this someone new?*

Stephen's methods didn't usually involve fire. Zion's passing made it even more unlikely that the creatures would have access to it. Making his way out of the school, he hoped he would find the answers. With soaked shoes, Ron emerged from the wreckage.

Back out on the lawn, Kip was interviewing a young girl with long black hair and a dress to match. The pair were getting frustrated with each other. "Hey," Ron interjected as he approached them. "What's going on?"

"He doesn't believe me!" she said. Ron wondered if Kip could hear the pain in her voice.

"What's your name?" Ron asked the girl, ignoring his partner's scoffing.

"Evrona."

"What doesn't he believe, Evrona?"

She hesitated. "He's accusing me of killing someone."

"I'm not, sir! I was asking why she had blood on her hands and clothes. I never said she did anything." *She feels guilty about something.*

"Evrona," Ron said, attempting to show compassion. "We aren't here to blame anyone. We're here to help. I believe you, but we need to know what happened. We need to hear it from everyone, so we can get a better picture of what happened here. Once we do that, we'll be able to find the people that did this and stop them. Please, you aren't in trouble, tell me what happened. Why are you covered in blood?"

Any girl Ron knew would have been crying. The other girls in the line-up were. This one was holding back her tears, he could see that. Maybe the smeared eyeliner down her cheeks hinted that she had no more left in her, or maybe this wasn't the worst part of the night for her. There was something she feared more than accusations of murder. She glanced over to the trees in the darkness.

"It was that boy's fault," she said. "The one that came here to test us. His name was Stephen. Michelle, Manny, and Aubrey were all standing where it came from. A black void thing. I don't know what to call it. Michelle was trying to stop it, I think. I'm not sure because when it reached me my mind went foggy, and it made me relive... It made it happen again. That tall blonde wasn't around, though. I stopped him." She looked at Ron with pleading eyes. "He's the one that attacked me first. Not out here, but in the school. That bitch asked if anyone would help take my clothes... and he was so willing... He got what he deserved. I didn't plan on it. The fog made me do it!"

"Evrona," Ron responded. She was beginning to get hysterical. He put his hands out and motioned for her to breathe along with him. Together they took a moment. "I can tell you don't want to tell us exactly what happened. That's fine. I think we've heard enough. We'll get you help. No one will hurt you anymore. Can we get some help?"

The last question was directed at the medics in the area. One of the young girls approached them. "What's wrong?" the medic asked.

"She needs attention," Ron told her. "Evrona, she's a doctor. You don't have to tell us what happened, but for your safety, please tell her what happened to you in the school. Forget about the others. She's here to help you."

The two young women walked toward one of the vans marked with the medic symbol. Ron looked down the line of teenagers. Only about twenty or so seemed to have made it out alive. What confused him was that double that amount were on the lawn dead when they first arrived. *Too many.*

"Was that the last one?" he asked Kip.

"Yeah, man," he responded. "They all told the same story. A regular school day turned to horror when Stephen announced over the intercom they were going to participate in some kind of test. Every single one of them also said there was some structure around the building keeping them in. I don't see it. Something else I thought was odd was that three new students joined today. I could believe maybe one new kid in the middle of the school year, but three? Something's off about that. One of the kids also reported that the bodies of the teachers were found in a classroom off of the main building. It seems like none of these kids saw an adult they recognized all day. I don't know how they didn't call the police after noticing that one."

"What about a timeline?" Ron asked, hoping for some good news.

"Sure," Kip replied. "School starts and morning classes are fairly normal. Lunch is where things start to take a turn for the worse. Apparently, there was a crown? I'm not clear about it, but some students fought over it. Notably, the three new students were involved. After lunch, Stephen performed a test on each individual classroom. Somehow this kid pulled off sealing each room and filling it with water as a timer for the tests. Each survivor knew that half of the classrooms passed their tests. That accounts for nearly two hundred casualties. Apparently, there was a power struggle after that. Aubrey and Manny, both new students that started today, had different ideas on how to handle the situation. Our friend Evrona said that Aubrey wanted to be cautious, while Manny wanted to take action."

"Do we know where Manny is now?" Ron asked.

"No," Kip continued. "I'm not clear about the details, but somehow Asteria found herself caught in the middle of it all. We both know how that ended. The survivors confirmed that Manny was the one that killed her. Then started shooting at students. It's also not clear where the gun came from. As of right now, its location is unknown as well. One thing they all agree on is none of them know why or how the gym blew up. They all heard the explosion and exited from there. Then you were here to hear part of what happened next. A dark dome surrounded the area and caused everyone to lose it. The kids turned on each other. We're left with twenty-four survivors."

"That makes this the highest casualty related incident," Ron said, concluding Kip's thoughts. "What was it that kid said? Something about a tall blonde? That didn't sound like she knew them. Was there anyone else described that way, or did anyone say anything about anyone without mentioning their name?"

Kip took a moment to think. "One of the girls had said something about a man with a wide smile. She also mentioned feeling dizzy around him." The two men looked at each other. The realization hit them at the same time.

"It can't be," Ron said in disbelief. "It was Edgar. The tall blonde must have been Tuls. She is the only one depraved enough to torture kids in that manner. If they're working together, this is bad. They've never been organized. We have to assume there were multiple creatures. It would explain how Stephen was able to execute something of this caliber."

"I thought those patients died in the fire at Pandora?" Kip asked apprehensively. Ron realized his mistake. He wasn't supposed to leak that they were still alive. The shock from knowing that at least two of them were here made his mind slip.

"Look, kid," Ron said to Kip. "Don't repeat what I'm about to tell you. Got it?" Kip nodded. "The official report is that all the patients died when Zion burned Pandora down along with himself. The truth is after Stephen was lost in his relocation processing, that boy went back and got all of his friends out. It's true Zion went down with the ship but not before releasing everyone. We assumed that they had all gone their separate ways. Castle can't admit that they lost every single creature, right? They'd lose all funding. Instead, they just said all the patients died and only Stephen was still lost. That way they could begin to search for the new receivers and Stephen while maintaining their credibility. This is bad. We never imagined they would work together."

The thought of the amount of paperwork all of this was going to accumulate crossed Ron's mind. Kip was left speechless. Ron was beginning to get a headache. Tracking multiple targets made it easier, sure, but that was always the easy part of the hunt. It was the fight they put up at the end that made it difficult. The siblings had notoriously been difficult, and they were kids at the time scared and confused. If three of the creatures from Pandora were together, was it even possible to capture them?

"Is anyone looking in the forest?" The question came from a young girl in the group of survivors. Her tone carried her anger for her.

"Why?" Kip asked.

"That's where they went."

"Who?" Ron asked, feeling like he already knew the answer.

"Michelle and Manny. They took off when we all heard the sirens. Stephen might have been the reason for all of this, but that Manny guy was a killer when he got here. He promised to kill Stephen for what he did to Mercy." Kip took his walkie and began to request their search team. "She was carrying something. It looked like a black flame. How can you carry fire in the palm of your hands?"

[10: 02 P.M.]

Epilogue

"THIS has never been done before," the outsider said. "In this world, there is a finite amount of soul. You all share it with each other through your interactions, through death, and through birth. When a person dies, their soul disperses into humans being born. You're predisposed to have a capacity to be human. Everyone begins with a varying amount of these human traits. Love, compassion, fear, apathy, manipulation. If you can think of it, most people contain some degree of it. You all have an imbalance. You all are different. You are made mostly of a single human trait. Aubrey was the first person I met. She was also like this. She had too much of what you'd call a need to protect inside her.

"Stephen was doubt personified. I don't need to tell you that, though. I know you all experienced it. The red fog, the black chains, and the fear of doubt, that was Stephen. This is Stephen. This black flame in my hands. I've controlled the flow of soul in small quantities, in mixtures and experiments, but I've never halted the natural redistribution of a decaying soul. Let alone one that was so pure of a single human trait."

"Can you bring him back?" The question came from Tuls, but each of them wanted to know.

The outsider looked her in the eyes. Then looked to Manny.

"I can," she responded. "We will need a vessel."

"Do you mean me?" Manny asked.

"It can be anyone," she continued. "To be clear, I don't know what will happen when we bring him back. I've never done this before."

"If I'm the only option, then I will proudly accept the responsibility."

Apart from Manny and the outsider, the other eleven seemed to agree. Stephen must be brought back.

The youngest in the group spoke up, "he saved us." She was a young girl with a soft voice to match. A large man stepped up to speak for the child. The man would make an excellent soldier, Manny found himself thinking.

"We owe him," the large man said. "Why are you so willing?"

"I've never felt I had a purpose," Manny responded. "My life has been filled with blood and scraps from people better than me. Stephen made me feel like I could prove I was worth saving. If I can help him, then I want to. Will I be me or will I be Stephen?" The question was for the outsider.

"Like I said," she replied. "I've never done this before. I don't know what will happen."

"We can't lose anyone else!" a scrawny dark man shouted from the shadows. His eyes held lies. The rest of the group joined in affirming the idea to place the fire inside of Manny.

"I'm ready," he said to the outsider. "Before we begin, though. Can I ask you something?" She nodded in response. "Why aren't you mad at me?"

"For what?" she asked.

"For killing Aubrey. She was your only friend. She protected you, going so far to try to kill me for you. You haven't mentioned her once."

"I've been alive for a long time," she responded with a somber tone. "I've seen the end of civilizations and generations of good people. Aubrey was a good person. When this is all over. I'll outlive you all. She was just another body of flesh destined to return to the dirt where she came from."

The room fell silent after this response. Manny felt hurt even. "Look," she continued. "I just want to go back home. Stephen said he can get me back there, and I believed him. You all want to survive this foretold apocalypse, right? And he said he can save you. He's already saved you from your prisons. We all have the same goal."

"Okay," Manny responded. He just wanted her to stop. The group was already convinced. "Do it."

"Lie on your back," she commanded. Manny did as he was told.

Inside the house, one that used to belong to one of the faculty members back at the school, Manny pushed the coffee table from the center of the living and laid down. The ceiling was adorned with beautiful molding and an expensive metal chandelier. The others moved to the entryway of the room. It led to a dark hallway that sprawled through the heart of the home. The outsider, Michelle, as they all began to call her, stood over Manny with the black flame.

She dropped it above his chest. It floated gently through the air, flickering the whole way. Just before it landed, the outsider pushed her hands on top of the wisps of the fire. A bright light emanated from her palms as she struggled to force the fire into Manny's body. The flame made contact and consumed his entire being.

The screams from Manny's pain and Michelle's effort filled the house. The fire seemed to come alive as it grew, spreading from Manny to Michelle. A wave of heat, as hot as the sun, washed over the onlookers. They all flinched to protect themselves. If someone had been walking by the house, it would be hard to convince them a train wasn't heading toward them. A roar of sparks and screams bounced around the house. In a flash of light, the fire siphoned to the young man's chest and then fell into him like the last bit of water leaving a draining sink. The room went back to normal.

Michelle rolled over onto the floor, breathing heavily. Manny was staring at the ceiling. He didn't look the same. It was like they all witnessed a new person be born before their eyes. Suddenly, he sat up and spoke.

"I can't see the future," the young man said. "I can't hear the screams. Where was I?"

Tuls ran to his side and said, "Stephen, you were gone, but she brought you back."

The young man looked at his hands and then at the girl unconscious on the carpet. Tuls was touching his skin, but she couldn't feel that same sense of insanity she was used to. She let go of his arm, becoming afraid. "Who are you?" she asked.

"I can feel two souls inside me," he responded. "I'm neither of them. I am consequence. I am doubt. Call me, Keller."

Acknowledgements

NONE of this would be possible without my wife, Kayla. She generously allows me to express my thoughts, questions, and feelings on absolutely everything. Hours and days go into reading and editing these stories. As they exist, they are as much hers as they are mine. My infinite soul is yours.

Made in the USA
Monee, IL
25 September 2023

43417786R00094